F
L97   Lustig, Arnost.
            Night and hope.

F
L97   Lustig, Arnost.
            Night and hope.

Temple Israel Library
Minneapolis, Minn.

———

Please sign your full name on the above card.

Return books promptly to the Library or Temple Office.

Fines will be charged for overdue books or for damage or loss of same.

CHILDREN OF THE HOLOCAUST

THE COLLECTED WORKS OF ARNOST LUSTIG

NIGHT AND HOPE

NIGHT AND HOPE

by Arnost Lustig

INSCAPE / PUBLISHERS / Washington, D. C.

Translated by
George Theiner

Copyright© 1976 by Arnost Lustig
Printed in the United States of America. All rights reserved.
No part of this book may be used or reproduced in any manner
whatsoever without written permission except in the case of
brief quotations embodied in critical articles and reviews.
For information address INSCAPE Corporation, 1629 K Street, N.W.,
Washington, D. C. 20006

Library of Congress Catalog Card Number 76-39999
International Standard Book Number: ISBN 0-87953-400-1

Library of Congress Cataloging in Publication Data
Lustig, Arnošt.
Night and hope.

(His Children of the Holocaust)
I. Title.
PZ4.L97Ni6[PG5038.L85] 891.8'6'35 76-39999
ISBN 0-87953-400-1

To fall, to rise a hundred times
and not to sigh!

Unknown Poet of the Terezín Ghetto

Contents

*

The Return

No, the relief he had expected to feel did not come. True,
it had been pretty bad in the alcove. But now he was out of
it, he had nowhere to go. He took an uncertain look along
the street and stopped abruptly. Walk, he told himself, as if
you were on your way to the tailor.

He started out again. Once he used to go like this to his
coffee-house, bowing slightly to acquaintances and knowing
that he was one of them. Now he felt his chin trembling. But
what could happen to him if he walked along, as he did now,
unassumingly treading an empty stretch of pavement? One
step – blue paving-stones, another step – white. He must not
be scared. What was there about him that anyone could
notice? He struggled against a constricting feeling of doubt.
The pressure in his temples called attention to itself by a
violent throbbing. Jew! a voice called somewhere inside him.
He was startled, was it his imagination, or did the houses on
either side of him give back an echo? His legs carried him
involuntarily off the pavement and into the gutter. But no, he
admonished himself, that was nonsense. He mounted the pavement once more. One step, blue, another step, white. Did he
have his money on him? With a feverish hand he felt his
pocket. Was it all there? His white, bony fingers, thickly grown
with black hairs spread out on the coat like a convulsed fan.
He sighed with relief, keeping his palm for a moment on the
spot where he could feel through the cloth the tough leather
of his wallet. He had forgotten something though; his lips! He
must not keep his mouth so tightly compressed. He remembered his moustache. The hand which had just by a mere

9

touch conveyed a morsel of tranquillity to the mind of the little man suddenly shot up to his lips, fingering the almost invisible triangle of a moustache. One step, blue paving stones, another step, white. And now the pavement was at an end. Was he to cross the street? Or should he go back? The echo of that last word reverberated inside him a thousand times and then faded into silence. Back – where? He crossed the street. He tried to visualize his own face, his thoughts again returning to the moustache. The moustache. He had shaved it two days ago, feeling that something would happen unless he did it. He had terrified the owner of the flat. What an idea! 'But you can't go out, Mr Tausig! It's daytime!' That was just why he had to go. The recess stifled him. A living being could not survive so long in the darkness of a recess scooped out of the kitchen wall and concealed by a sideboard. He simply had to go out, and that was why he had shaved. He had shaved deliberately slowly. A smell of marzipan hovered about the room. A round, white, blue-edged clock mechanically and unfeelingly ticked away the time. He washed the white lather off his face and dried himself with his handkerchief because he did not want to bother anyone for a towel. The elderly couple who sheltered him watched him anxiously, horrified by the thought that at that very moment someone would come rushing into their kitchen. They pulled the blinds down; the day changed into a grey semi-darkness. 'We haven't any children, Mr Tausig, but we should still like to live to see the end of the war.' There was nothing he could say. It seemed to him that with his moustache gone, he had lost his face. He crept back into his recess, and no longer rapped with his knuckles on the back of the sideboard. They would suffer with him, that was the trouble. The end of the war, he thought, when is that coming?

Hynek Tausig stroked his moustache with his finger-tips. A car's klaxon hooted some distance away. There was a smell of marzipan there, he recalled, while he had been shaving. And someone had talked about the end of the war. In a car which he could not see someone was now driving somewhere, someone who knew where he was going. Some people had hope, others had nothing. Nothing at all. One step – blue paving-stones, another step – white. His eyes surveyed the familiar patterns of the paving. As a child he used to pick his way carefully so as to step only on the blue stones. That, he had believed, brought luck. He must not even now tread on the white ones. One step, blue, another step, blue. He must make bigger strides. If he did not step on the white perhaps every-thing would turn out well. What about his wallet? He dropped his hands once more, the right pressing his hip. He ought not to be so scared. Better keep his arm there. But was that not too conspicuous? He let his arms drop alongside his body. Perhaps it would be a good idea to hide part of his money somewhere. But where was he to find a suitable place, a place he could go back to any time he needed? No, he decided, he would not hide it anywhere. If the Gestapo caught him, he would not return anywhere, in any case.

The small man was suddenly at a loss what to do with his hands. He tried putting them in his pockets, but was im-mediately startled by the thought that if he were to meet sol-diers they might think he held a weapon there. He pulled his hands out abruptly as if they had been licked by some invis-ible flame. He crossed the street, Careful, he commanded him-self, not so fast! Do you want to get into trouble for jaywalking! How stupid of him! He must not do that again.

Someone was walking straight at him. He swerved aside, his eyes diffidently gliding over the stranger's face. The face was unknown to him. Its image, however, remained in front of his eyes even though they were now peering at the ground as if searching for something there. He could see that face all the time, and now he was no longer so sure that it was un-known. A blue stone, a white. There was something familiar about it . . . Not the white. Blue, blue again, and another blue. He must not think about it, that was asking for bad luck. His eyes bored into the paving. Now, in a flash, he saw that all his fond imaginings of the night before were nothing but a lot of hooey – the idea that he would feel better in the street than in his recess, that the city was life whereas the recess was death, the street light and the hole in the wall night, and that nobody would recognize him because he had run to seed. Nothing was better. Neither the fact that he had shaved, nor the fact that his moustache had slightly grown again. Neither the recess, nor the street. He bent forward over the pavement and walked on in this hunchback fashion. At least no one could see his face. A small, comforting certainty. A man walking in the opposite direction was close to him. They passed. All he saw were black shoes, frayed trouser cuffs of a rough, grey material, and dried particles of mud. How was he to judge whether it was someone he knew from a little mud on grey trousers? He badly needed a little certainty. But whatever he did, he must not turn round. He stepped carefully only on the blue stones. Perhaps it was not anybody he knew, after all. But if it was and the man had not recognized him, then he might do so if he were to turn round now. Blue, blue, blue. He would go crazy. His head! But why was he walking along the main avenue all the time? If he did meet anyone he knew, he could easily pretend he was not who he really was, nor even what he was, but – how ridiculously little for twenty thousand! – Alfred Janota, engineer of a boiler-making firm in Hradec Králové. Blue, blue. He had an identity card to prove it. Black on white. Alfred Janota. Blue. His skull was sure to crack with the pain. But he must not turn round.

Blue. He must convince himself in the first place that he no longer had anything in common with Hynek Tausig. Did you say Tausig? Oh, dear me, no. I would not have anything to do with him. It sounds so terribly Jewish! Wasn't he some kind of commercial traveller? He felt like laughing, but only his chin shook. Tausig was Janota. What a comedy. Could he really believe it, though? If they hauled him off to the Petschek Palace, they would soon beat it out of his head, together with his teeth. Blue, blue. But he, Hynek Tausig, really was Alfred Janota. The identity card was genuine. He had paid twenty thousand for it. It bore the rubber stamp of the police headquarters of Prague's third precinct and the signature of a

police official. Here was Tausig and here was Janota. A quick
exchange. Here was money and here was an identity card.
Blue. What a transaction! How many times in one's life did
one do it? For one's own money one became someone else.
Blue, blue. He ought to take himself away somewhere and sit
down. That man could not have known him, or he would
have been back a long time ago. Blue. If only there were a
lawn somewhere near. Cool, springy grass. He longed to be
able to plunge his elbows into it and to rest his head in his
hands. Formerly, he could do this any time he liked. To support his head, before it burst into fragments. He turned away
from the main avenue.

A little way off he reached a backwater. A quiet street
enveloped in a blue veil of receding mist. There was nobody
about. His eyes registered a deserted building site and, in front
of him, a pub. A good job he had come away from the busy
thoroughfare. Squirrels carved by Italian stone-masons
chased each other on the double stone portal of 'The Green
Huntsman'. It was an ancient house, an ancient pub. How
about slipping in? The men who were just having their
elevenses inside were doubtless workmen from the building
site opposite. What time was it? Ten. The sight of people
drove away the serenity of the quiet street. It suddenly seemed
to him that the bricklayers inside there did not build flats.
They built nothing but recesses, thousands of them. He felt
sick. He circled the inn. No curtains in the windows, so that
you could see into everyone's stomach, what they were eating
and what they were drinking. Who was that leaning against
the bar counter? And whose was the hat with a feather hanging on the wall? Any uniforms? No – no uniforms. 'The
Green Huntsman'. What a funny name. Like Janota. But better. A huntsman was a huntsman. And green at that. Nothing
more. No pretence about it. Just a green huntsman. What if
one of the guests was a Vlajka man? Well, what if he was, Mr
Janota? he heard something say inside him. Why should you
care? You have a tongue to speak with, haven't you. How are
you? A member of the Vlajka, eh? Oh yes, a meritorious or-

ganization that. It will rid us of the Jewish menace. And, who knows, perhaps sooner than our friends from the Reich. I knew a Jew once, too. Name of Tausig. Hynek Tausig. He travelled in vacuum cleaners. No, he was quite alone in the world, no relatives. Good, Mr Janota. You're one of us. One can tell, you know, as soon as you open your mouth. Blue. Well, how about it, would he dare to go in at last, or not? It must look suspicious, hanging about like this. He felt someone looking at him from inside. Someone was looking him over. Two penetrating human telescopes. Serve him right! Why did he have to moon about in front of the door so long? Either he must go in or go away. But he did not feel in the least decisive. On the contrary, a wave of self-pity surged over him. If only they had curtains there, nobody would have seen him. Everything conspired against him. What good did it do him that he was so down at the mouth and that no one would recognize him? Anyone with his haggard look was sure to be under suspicion these days.

He turned back to the speckled stones bordering the pavement, longing desperately to lie down on one of them. If only he could press his face and forehead against the stone, the weariness that weighed him down would leave him. He would surely go to sleep, and that would be a blessing. The pavement. Suddenly everything he had ever known was narrowed down to the oblong of speckled stone. Here he had been born and here he had lived – forty years already. It had all been but one long day, and now it was evening and he was about to lie down. Heavens! It was only an hour since he had gone out into the streets. Perhaps it would be better to go into the pub, after all. Order an ale and a cucumber, standing up by the bar. But weren't cucumbers rationed now? He forgot to ask in the morning. He saw in his mind's eye the white kitchen clock with its blue border and felt a pang of home-sickness. They used to have a similar clock at home. Mother used to wind it and she never forgot. And what about beer – was that rationed or not? He had some ration coupons with him. He pulled out his wallet. Where were they? After he had feverishly fingered through all the compartments his anxiety turned to certainty; he must have lost them! There, what a blow!

The door creaked and there were voices. Blue tunics smeared with white. The bricklayers came swarming out, their break over. Their questioning glances crushed him. One of them gave him a friendly slap on the shoulder. 'Had one over the eight, chum?' He staggered under the impact of a huge, hard hand. Mustn't fall, he thought desperately, steady! That would be suspicious. The eyes of one of the men seemed hostile, as if he were saying: how comes that anyone has money for booze nowadays? If only he could do something about it and stop people from looking at him!

Why had he not stayed where he was, in that wretched hole? But how could he? They did not like to see him go out, even at night. Pass the bucket and see that the handle does not rattle, take it back again, and that was all. Why did the chap ask if he had had one over the eight? What were they thinking about, anyway? Cognac, of course. Maybe it was just a test. Now they would come back, one of them would turn up his lapel and show him the badge, and they would lead him off. And then – he heard the concrete mixer start into action; thank God, they were just bricklayers. Nobody was going to lead him anywhere.

He walked on with a feeling of impending doom. A trap would suddenly be sprung and he would go hurtling down through a trapdoor without even knowing what had happened. He must not enter that inn. He must not enter any public place. Somebody would make a silly remark and they would pick all of them up, him as well. Then perhaps they might even let the others go, but he would be caught. They were good at these things and knew how to do them on a large scale; a whole tramload of people, a whole street, a whole everything.

He was in Karlín. If he carried on like this, neither slow nor fast, he would be in Wenceslas Square within ten minutes. That was something entirely different. There he would not have to walk like a ram with head bent low. The Square,

that was his first aid post; transfusion, density – nobody took
any notice of anybody else. Excuse me, or pardon, I'm in a
hurry. If it had not been for those three weeks in that recess,
he would not be so terrified. He would get over it soon. There,
you see, Hynek, old fellow, he said to himself encouragingly,
it is better outside, after all. Who on earth would imagine that
the little chap who would shortly be walking in Wenceslas
Square was anybody but Alfred Janota?

Blue, blue. Three weeks spent among suitcases and gazing
into the darkness unless he wished to suffocate with the stench
of petroleum. And hearing all the time: 'For heaven's sake,
Mr Tausig, be careful and don't set it alight!' There was that
danger on top of everything else. Blue. He would have burned
to death behind the sideboard. Thin wood, piles of paper,
cardboard – and he, a mere cinder. The thought of the recess
made him feel sick, though at the same time he was conscious
of relief at being out in the fresh air. Blue. He would soon be
in the centre of the city.

Soldiers! That was the end. The trap had been sprung. They
were coming towards him, taking up practically the entire
width of the pavement. Quickly, to the edge, he commanded
himself. How was he to behave? You are Janota, you idiot,
Janota, Janota, Janota! Perhaps he should smile. But not too
conspicuously. A grimace appeared on his ashen-coloured
face. The men in the green field uniforms took no notice of
him, however. They passed by a nonentity which did not
realize that it was enough to remove oneself to the edge of
the pavement and that it was not necessary to step right down
into the gutter. He breathed with relief. But immediately afterwards he stiffened, the grimace still distorting his face. He
heard a voice and felt someone's breathing. 'Hey, what's the
time?' Here it was. Did Alfred Janota understand German?
That was all he could think of. He pushed back his sleeve a
little to enable the returned soldier to look at the dial of his
watch. But it was not he who was doing it, somebody else
inside him was responsible for the action. 'Damn,' he heard,
'a quarter past ten. Bags of time yet.' They were walking some

way ahead, loud and rowdy, and the last one, the one who had come back to ask him the time, was hurrying to catch up with them. Hynek Tausig was aware only of the variegated pattern of the pavement and of nothing else. The only thing he knew was that he must not stop if he did not want to collapse. Blue.

He met increasingly more people now. There, he assured himself, there will be whole crowds of them in Wenceslas Square. He went alternately faster and again more slowly. He was not used to so much walking. He stopped to rest at the street corner. His eyes sought and found the red board with white lettering. It was pleasant to see that the street was still called Príkopy as it used to be. In a minute he would be at the 'Koruna'. There he would find a buffet and a public baths. He had been three weeks without a bath. But that would be dangerous; he would have to hand in everything he had on him – his identity card and his money. He would be given a locker and a key. But what if they had another? And anyway, were the baths still there? Again he felt his pocket anxiously. The money was there. Blue.

He should have something to eat, too. Not that he was hungry. But he ought to eat or he would find himself fainting through weakness. He ought to get his change ready in advance. A new anxiety flared up within him – the wallet was there all right, but was the money still in it? He must take a look at once or he would go crazy.

A newsman was standing on the corner of Príkopy and Wenceslas Square, leaning against the wall, his crutch and bag full of newspapers lying on the ground in front of him. He was looking at the passers-by in a perfunctory manner, a mere glance here and there. But if someone took his fancy, he would pick him out of the crowd and rivet him with his eyes. The pale man timidly asking for a sports paper seemed very unsure of himself. Why was he speaking in such a low voice? There was something behind it. What other paper, though, could be demanded by an Alfred Janota whom it would suffice to turn upside down and shake slightly for Hynek Tausig to fall out? Nothing that was not non-commit-

B

tal, nothing political, no news – all that did not interest him. The weight fell off his shoulders; the money was there. But why ever did he fold it in such an impossible way. He had to take out a fifty-crown note. Would the man have change? He felt like leaving him with the whole fifty crowns and walking away. That fellow was scanning him much too closely. Fortunately he did have change. The man saw nothing unusual in being paid with such a high denomination. People needed change and a newsman came in handy. What was the matter with his customer though? A queer tyke. The news vendor was counting out the change, his voice slightly ahead of his hands. He could see that the rum bloke who had bought the newspaper off him was absent-minded. How about giving him a few hellers less? Then he changed his mind; that ashen face with the hint of a moustache did not look at all prosperous. He gave him the correct change: one crown, ten, fifty. As likely as not, thought the news vendor, he is a Jewboy.

Hynek Tausig's hair was bluish-black, but his nose was straight and thin like a Spanish aristocrat's. Perhaps his ancestors had in actual fact come from there, fleeing the *auto-da-fé,* just as he, their descendant, would like to escape from here. So far, however, he had not done more than cross the threshold. He had only not joined the transport, had not presented himself at the Sample Fair palace, the first stop on the way to the ghetto at Terezín. The knowledge did not give him any satisfaction. Had he gone, it occurred to him, he might now have been left in peace. Whereas now, what were his prospects: getting his teeth knocked out, a bullet or a rope, or, at best, again the ghetto. Why did he not feel admiration for himself for having dared to stay away? He had heard a lot about Hitler even before his troops had marched into Prague. It had never occurred to him to put up any resistance. But for some incomprehensible reason he had thought that his straight nose would enable him to shed what was known as his Jewish origin. That was the only lever he had used to upset it all. He had torn up the small white paper they had sent to summon him to the transport. In the evening he had left his flat – and the transport had left without him.

What an advantage it was, he thought as he patted his pocket once more, what an advantage that he looked like Janota now that it was so essential. Had anyone told him what the news vendor had thought, he would not have believed it possible. He walked on. Although he considered the money he had to be the sum total of his means of escape, its possession failed to give him a feeling of contentment. There was something that disturbed him, but he could not discern what it was.

At last he reached Wenceslas Square. He was conscious of a certain disappointment that the rectangles of paving were exactly the same as in Príkopy. Nor was it as crowded here as he had imagined it would be as he walked along the streets of Karlín. No, no press of people in which to hide. He would like to stop and look round, but he went on without doing either. After all, he had not lost his wits. So many soldiers about! He crossed to the other side of the street, but could not find what he was looking for even there. He fixed desperate eyes on the equestrian statue of St Wenceslas at the top of the Square – it seemed terribly small and insignificant, and it came to him with sudden force that he had been deceiving himself all the time he was hurrying to get here. And, moreover, had known he was deceiving himself at the very moment he had left the house. He had simply run away from the recess. It's the same everywhere, Hynek Tausig, he whispered to himself, here or there, it's all one. A big mess with a thousand holes. You were bound to step in one of them, you would fall in, and you would never make the fresh air again. The clanging of the trams jarred on his ears, seeming like mockery. 'Well, well, Mr Tausig,' the red cars seemed to jeer, 'still travelling in vacuum cleaners? How about boarding a twenty-two and jumping off at the statue – head first?'

The saint's statue appeared to him sombre and hostile. He turned his back on it. He was tired out. Should he try the baths? Who was to decide? It was noon, possibly there would be nobody there. He would go and wash off his fear. Then he would get into the steam, climb up on the plank, lie on his back, and, having sweated profusely, take a lukewarm shower. Then he would give the attendant a little money to let him take a nap. All right, he would go. Come what may. He stepped out faster. But before he was half-way down the Square he had lost most of his courage. Don't tremble, he admonished himself. Tausig would be left behind in the baths, only Janota would come out. However, by the time he had reached the bottom of the Square he knew he would never enter the baths. Yet, in spite of that, he shuffled along right to the entrance. A voice said: 'Need any cigarettes?' A pair of inquisitive eyes rested on his face. Cigarettes? He shook his head in negation. No, he did not need any cigarettes, but why did the fellow look at him so searchingly? Tausig in his turn looked harder at the man, to find out what he was like. A clean-shaven face, everything in it pointed: the eyes, the nose, and the ears, even the cheek-bones. No, the face did not appeal to him. He ought to say, 'Beat it, pal,' or 'Don't bother me or I'll call a policeman!' But he would say nothing, he would merely walk on. Yet, his feet seemed glued to the spot. That fellow held him in some inexplicable way. Perhaps he should tell him, after all. Perhaps that would drive him away. But what if the man was an *agent provocateur*: perhaps he had picked him as a victim and was trying it out on him. And if he asked: 'How much are they?' or 'Give me five packets of ten . . .' he would produce a card and take him to headquarters. No, he could not say either the one or the other, for a variety of reasons.

The pointed face had a brain of its own. Taking in the ashen-grey countenance, the haunted eyes and the drooping mouth of the man facing him, he thought that here was a possibility, a definite possibility. This – he thought, appraising the small figure in front of him – was no small minnow, this was likely as not a fat big trout. He came right up to the little man and said: 'I shan't squeal, never fear. I'm on the run, too.'

Should he perhaps fall on his knees now and just beg for mercy, Tausig wondered. Surely he could not end like this? But then, did he, Hynek Tausig, not realize that he could not, the times being what they were, simply up and go for a walk? Just like that. Where would he have gone anyway, had he not met pointed-face? What was he thinking of, actually, when he left his own flat four weeks ago? The man said he was 'on the run' too. What did he mean by it? That he was a 'submarine' like him, Hynek Tausig? Or that he had no money? Or did he merely want to pump him? He would have to ask him to let him go, tell him that he was in a hurry. They themselves were forcing him to act like this. But whatever happened, he must not break down now, must not show the man how desperately scared he was. He moved. At last he brushed past pointed-face, calling out to him 'What d'you want?' as he went. What *did* he want? Whatever it was, he was going. If the man wanted him to show his identity card, well, all right, why not? He had his papers in order, and they were made out in the name of Janota.

But pointed-face caught up with him. 'Let me have a hundred, won't you, pal. I'm in the same fix as you.'

The two pairs of eyes met: a watery, greyish-green pair with a vigilant gleam in them, with the brown, inquiring, burning, heavy-lidded and seemingly ash-covered, disturbed eyes of Hynek Tausig. If he but knew that a hundred crowns would rid him of pointed-face, he would give them to him. At forty, Hynek Tausig was fundamentally the same as he had been at fifteen, at twenty, and at thirty: settle everything peacefully. Yes, if he knew it for sure, he would give the money to him and be done with it. But he could not pull out his wallet in front of his eyes, so, in a quiet voice, he said only: 'Where would I get them from?'

The tone of his voice betrayed him, however. Pointed-face stepped squarely in front of him. 'You miser, leave a pal to stew in his own juice while you make your own get-away, would you?' he hissed.

Good Lord, was it possible that the man could read his

thoughts? But pointed-face did not, of course, think that Hynek Tausig was somebody who ought to be wearing a yellow star, he simply had the impression that this small, pale and tired-looking fellow was in the same line of business as he and that he was at the moment in difficulties. Otherwise what would he be doing here? Why should he be standing in front of the entrance to the baths – and not go in? And so, if only he could keep up this battle of nerves a few moments longer, Hynek Tausig would win through after all.

All he did now was to whisper: 'What d'you want of me? I haven't got anything.' Why did that man block his way like this? Damned cheek, anyway. And someone might see them. He said, more loudly this time: 'Go away! Don't bother me!' This last in a shrill voice that sounded as if it were forced out of him. He was seized by doubts whether it would not be better to implore, after all.

A policeman came into sight at the bend of the passage. Things were quite different now. Hynek Tausig had to take a step forward in order not to stand directly opposite pointed-face. 'A copper!' he hissed. And pointed-face vanished with all the speed that Hynek Tausig could have wished for right at the start, when he was meditating about the baths. The policeman was gazing at the receding back of pointed-face and he passed Hynek Tausig quietly, taking not the slightest notice of him, walking past with an easy, rolling gait which somehow gave the impression that for all his apparent nonchalance he was alert and ready for action.

So much for the baths, thought Hynek Tausig, trying to centre his attention on this and nothing else. The glimpse he had had of the policeman brought back to him the whole hopelessness of his situation. There, on one side of the fence, was the law – what of it that it was a law that would not pass muster in front of any real justice – and there, on the other side of the fence, was he, a human being beyond the pale, an outlaw. If he managed to get into the baths, it would all be different. In his imagination he conjured up the water, almost feeling the soothing warmth of it as it ran over his body. Then it came, suddenly – the realization that he could not possibly go in there. How could he have forgotten! A straight nose was not everything if he did not have his trousers on. He was Alfred Janota only in his clothes. Without them, he was demonstrably Hynek Tausig. He was Alfred Janota only on the outside, not inside. Had he gone in, he might have paid for it very unpleasantly. Come to think of it, it was a good thing that he had been detained by that tramp. He thought of his mother's favourite adage: something bad for something good. But he was annoyed with his parents – by having him circumcised they had spoiled his chances of a bath. Immediately he forgot the reasons that had a minute ago prevented him from going on down, feeling on the contrary sad and sorry for himself that he was now unable to enter the baths at all.

He entered the buffet instead. It was hot inside and the air was bad. The close, sultry atmosphere somehow reminded him of his recess. Two SS men were standing by the shiny beer counter, having drinks poured out for them. At the food stall some soldiers were lunching on *schnitzels,* standing up. He swallowed. Oh, the swine, he thought, devouring everything. He crossed over to a large board that read 'Off the Ration'.

Wasn't he conspicuous ordering soup? Decent people were sure to have at least a few food coupons on them. But he was not the only one. One crown twenty. At least this time he would give the correct change. A girl with eyes the colour of forget-me-nots and with red hands, slightly swollen from the steam, was serving; she scooped up the soup out of the pot and, handing him the plate, said, 'There you are.' Looking at her, he thought she reminded him of a flower, something pure – her voice, however, brought him back to earth. It was irritable, impatient and rather surly. But why? Could such a girl denounce him? Her eyes no longer seemed so clear and pure, no resemblance to forget-me-nots. I've not given her the money! it occurred to him. Of course, that was it – he had forgotten to pay. He must put it right immediately. He attempted an apologetic smile, but only a twisted grin

appeared on his face. The girl was convinced that the little
man had tried to swindle her, and she made no secret of her
conviction. She pouted her lips. I know your kind, they
seemed to be saying. Hynek Tausig ate his soup, feeling the
girl's eyes in the small of his back. Eat it up quickly and get
out! He ate hurriedly, scalding his tongue and throat, but
he knew he had to be quick. The girl might call someone in
the meantime. Better leave the soup unfinished. He left the
plate on the high table, at which there were several other
patrons. As he pushed his way out, someone caught hold of
his arm. So here it was. He had known it was coming. He had
felt it in the air. Behind him he heard a dull, embarrassed
voice. He turned round slowly. It had all been quite hopeless
from the start. He had told the people who had sheltered him
that he had friends in the country and in Prague too, that if
he did not manage to get out of town, he would spend the
night with them. Did he lie when he said that, or did he
believe it himself? He no longer knew. The hand which had
grasped hold of him had been relaxed, the voice was saying
something. 'I'm terribly sorry, I thought it was Ferdinand.'
The man departed with an apology, leaving Hynek Tausig
standing there, wiping the perspiration from his brow. It was
moist. Beads of sweat were streaming down his cheeks. He felt
sticky all over. He was confronted by the image of someone's
life, a troublesome life perhaps, but still a life – the life of
someone called Ferdinand, who could meet a friend and the
friend would be pleased by the coincidence.

He opened the glass door and emerged into the street. He
was possessed by the harassing feeling that unless he immediately, without delay, got out into the suburbs, he would be
caught here. Passing a florist's shop with nothing in the window but a single Chinese vase with red roses in it and with
mirrors in the background, he had a glimpse of himself. God,
he could not walk bent like this. He looked at the roses. They
were still in the bud. A young couple came out of the shop,
the boy not more than eighteen, the girl probably even
younger. He, Hynek Tausig, would doubtless be older than

the two of them put together. They walked out, seeing no one in the whole Square but each other, the boy carrying a flower pot wrapped in white tissue paper. The girl had her arm around his waist. It looked rather ridiculous because of their overcoats. But the two evidently did not mind, this or anything else. He followed them with his eyes until they disappeared from sight in a cluster of people at the corner. They had somewhere to go all right, and they walked along without even thinking about it. Somewhere there was a house with a roof, an entrance and a staircase, a white or blue door with a bell, and a room or some tiny garret with two chairs, a bed and a table. And he had nothing – not even a ghost of anything of the sort.

2

An hour later the caretaker of 'The Fountain', a house in Siegfried Street in the Nusle district of Prague, saw Hynek Tausig ring the bell of a third-floor flat. The flat belonged to a childless married couple, he a buyer for a small store and she a cashier in a café. Hynek Tausig was at the end of his tether. He did not notice the caretaker, thinking as he ascended the stairs that it might be best to report at a police station and ask to be included in the next transport. He found it difficult to understand why he had not actually done it already. But he had been busy trying to find a way out. Surely he must have some friends somewhere. Somewhere he must have them. If not, there was only the police station left, or – no, he veered away from the thought, somewhere he *must* have some good friends. Then, when he was passing through Nusle, he had suddenly remembered this house. It rose up in front of him as if it had never been here before and had only just appeared. Something told him, though, that he ought to cross out these people as he had crossed out all the others whom he had thought of. He pressed the brown button of the bell. The buzzing noise had not died down inside and he was already wondering whether he should not go away before anyone came to open the door. Somewhere deep inside him there crouched at the same time the fear that the door would not even be opened on his account. What was he to say? That he was paying them a courtesy visit? Or: 'Could you lend me some salt?' Or again: 'Thought I'd drop in for a moment.' That was what people said. But there was a far worse possibility – that he would have nothing to say.

A man suddenly appeared in the doorway. He had calm grey eyes, slightly distended with surprise. Now his eyes were calm no longer – quickly they darted across the chest of the little man standing outside. And he understood the meaning of that swift glance: they were looking for a yellow star.

The caretaker was dusting the window-frames on the landing below. It was only now, as he peered nervously from side to side, that Hynek Tausig caught sight of her. What was he to do, he could not possibly talk in front of her. At the same time he knew that he would hardly be able to confide in those grey eyes. The caretaker was going down, her slippers clacking on the stairs. Some people were lucky – they could come out just so, in slippers. Hynek Tausig felt that unless he leaned against the door-post he would surely fall. How long had he been standing here? The caretaker was downstairs at last and silence returned to the house.

He stared at the white card on the door with the name of the owner of the flat printed on it. And that man, whose name was there tidily set out in the middle of a brass frame, stood in the doorway, still without saying a word. He was silent and waited. His thoughts were going round like a wheel; if the wheel stopped, he would ask Hynek Tausig to come in. He even felt inclined to say something nice and friendly to him, regardless of the fact that he had been seen by the caretaker and that such visits were dangerous these days. He could see without being told that the visitor needed support. But the wheel did not stop, taking with it all his determination as it revolved down the stairs, down the same stairs on which a moment ago clattered the caretaker's slippers. The wheel revolved with increasing speed, revealing something that filled the man in the doorway with horror. His mind focused on the picture of a party of SS men who had beaten his wife and himself for a single unfriendly look. That was last May, when they were searching for the perpetrators of the attempt on Heydrich's life. In his own grey eyes the man in the doorway now resembled an empty husk.

'What is it you want?' he asked.

Hynek Tausig went cold all over. Here it was. Though it was also possible that the man did not remember him. He ought to tell him that they had once worked together. That he had once helped him when his wife needed treatment at Franzensbad. That he had had a doctor acquaintance and everything had turned out well. Still, he had known this would happen. Anything would be better than to be standing here like this. Even a bullet in the head. But perhaps those grey eyes were really only looking him over. After all, he was shabby, his moustache a mere half-hearted bristle. Should he himself tell him who he was and what he wanted? His lips could not form the words. Go on, he urged himself, say it. But his tongue seemed wooden. Something emanated from that flat which stunned him and robbed him of the power of speech.

'I am Tausig,' he groaned. There, it was out!

'What do you want?' the man demanded. 'I'm busy.'

Something was pressing Hynek Tausig down, making him one with the dust on the red tiles of the floor. The caretaker would come and wipe him off with a wet rag and squeeze him out into a bucket full of dirty water. Why had he come here? He should not have done it. The door closed, the man with the grey eyes that had lost their tranquillity disappeared, the catch of the patent lock rattled like a thing that fitted perfectly in its place.

He glanced down over the banisters. Taking hold of the rail he shuffled down the stairs. Again he saw those grey eyes in front of him, searching for the star. There was no star, but the door had been closed just the same. Wasn't it really there? Or was it perhaps a star that could not be removed with a penknife?

Out in the street, he was seized by a depressing feeling of uselessness. His head seemed to him like a boiler in which something terribly insipid was being boiled over and over, something that would never taste right again. He still had his identity card. And nothing else. People walked about as if there were no war on. For them, he thought, war meant only marmalade instead of butter, lousy cigarettes, and rotten beer. He had to sit down. He could see himself, a stray dog running about the streets. There was no room anywhere for the likes of him. At the stop outside the park he boarded a tram.

The conductor let the ashen-faced man travel twice across town, from one terminus to the other and back again. When they stopped at one end he offered him coffee out of his thermos flask. 'Help yourself,' he said nonchalantly. Tired and sleepy, Hynek Tausig looked at him with distrust in his eyes. Coffee? 'Thanks.' He would take a drink first. The cup was hot. How pleasant to be able to hold it in his fingers like this. Should he trouble his head wondering whether the donor wished to denounce him? Had he bought a ticket this time? No, he hadn't. He had travelled free. He studied the conductor's tranquil face, a wise and at the same time slightly rough face. The conductor. Fiftyish. He gave the impression of belonging in that old red trailer car. Tausig had formerly taken little notice of conductors, one never knew whether they would turn out kind or grumpy. But how could this one have guessed that the best service he could do him, Hynek Tausig, at the present moment was to offer him some coffee? Would he denounce him afterwards? He finished his cup. 'Thank you,' he said. Should he get off? But where was he to go? The conductor leaned towards him and said something in a confidential tone. Did he hear right? Was the man telling him to sit down in a corner and take a nap? He was on duty till four in the morning. 'That's a lot of time, chum, almost all night.' 'Yes,' he replied. He sat down. He was terribly sleepy. Did he intend to denounce him? Sleepier and sleepier. Or didn't he?

The conductor watched the man as he dozed. I guess, he told himself, he's one of those that the street loudspeakers are always bawling about. Yesterday afternoon he had heard one such announcement right outside the Nusle Park where this man had got on. It was as if a huge glass bowl were smashed: crash, and then the harsh voice: sentenced to death for giving shelter to . . . No, he checked himself, chasing away thoughts of caution, these people need a helping hand these days.

And thus Hynek Tausig sat huddled in the corner of the tram car, drowsing until four in the morning. Then he got out at the terminus, having been given two large slices of bread and marmalade, a thermos full of tea, and another slice wrapped in newspaper. 'Thank you.' That was all, he did not even shake hands in his hurry. He walked back along the route of the 19 tram, which he had travelled five times to and fro.

3

The next day Hynek Tausig could be seen strolling about round the Sample Fair palace, bent forward just the same as yesterday, his ashen-coloured face a shade darker, whispering: blue. But the meaning of this word had been lost long ago. His bloodshot eyes bore into the concrete cube with its thousand eyes and with a huge collar formed by the wooden fence. The Prague quarter of Holešovice. Who would ever have thought that a part of the city would become the bridge over which people who had no business here would send live contingents to the transit point of another world, to the Prague-Bubny railway station.

A few minutes ago he had emerged out of a barber's shop. The barber had been a merry fellow, a homespun wit. Still, he was glad he was out of there. The police might come in and pick up such a wag any time, and the game would be up. No, the barber had not managed to cheer up his early customer who had come to have his moustache shaved off, however much he might have thought the little man needed cheering up. Hynek Tausig had had his moustache shaved off. At least nobody would recognize him now. But he knew very well that after the experience of yesterday it was completely useless to try and convince himself of this.

He came up close to the fence. He could hear quite distinctly the bustle in the warehouse where the Jews were gathering before being taken off to Terezín. He was possessed by the single overpowering wish: to get in among them. To be one of that yellow-branded herd. He would lose his freedom and *they* would treat him according to their habit, and that – he knew – would be anything but pleasant. In spite of that there was nothing he craved more at the moment. There He had seen them swarming there from a top floor window in were three thousand of them, or even more, behind that fence. the passage of the house opposite. He could imagine the smell – they were lying there packed like sardines, on mattresses and without them, on the floor sprinkled with wood shavings and strewn with straw. And yet he wished he could be lying among them, with his number on a label. As he looked on he also saw the SS beating people when the food was doled out. And yet he envied them, for they had a place of their own. If only he could stand there with them!

He thought only of how to get in there. He had not the slightest doubt that once he was inside, he would somehow manage to get taken along with the others. He saw people coming up to the fence when the policeman had passed by on his way round, and talking to someone through the gaps between the planks. He saw an old woman who stood leaning against the fence, perhaps talking to somebody or again perhaps just looking on. Whom might she have there – a husband or a son? But how can she be outside, it occurred to him, if they are in? The woman had red, swollen eyes, which she now dried with a white handkerchief. The policeman had passed by several times, curious rather than zealous. He had not said a word to her as yet, had not chased her away. He stood beside her now and listened. She had not seen him, so he gazed at the gap next to hers, trying to see with whom the woman was conversing. But he could not see anyone, only a thick mass of humanity, people lolling about on the ground and marked with stars and numbers on their luggage. She is probably calling all of them at once, thought the policeman. He must have been right, for until he told her to go away, she kept on weeping and addressing someone who was evidently one of that thousand-headed multitude with numbers.

I must get in there, Hynek Tausig murmured to himself, right in there. There was sweat on the palms of his hands. He was not hungry, not tired. He knew what he wanted. He knew what he was waiting for. And he waited. With the coming of dusk everything grew quiet. A German policeman took the place of the Czech one for the night. But he did not behave with any greater vigilance than his predecessor. Hynek Tausig inspected the uneven top of the fence. I'll simply run up to the fence and jump over, he told himself. No, better climb up and drop down on the other side. And though it looked quite easy in the dark, he knew at once that he would not be able to do it. What was it like in front of the entrance? Of course! He must go and have a look at the wooden staircase. He was taken by a new idea: walk quickly past the guards. They were standing there, lazy and inattentive. On the other hand that would mean he would have to stand here all night. Someone might notice him. He could also go straight to the policeman when he was alone and slip some money in his pocket. But no, policemen probably had all they needed. And then – would a policeman believe him? Could he dare try and spin him such a yarn? What – you didn't feel like it four weeks ago, did you? Here you are – a slap in the face and a bullet to go with it. No, he decided, that was out too.

He moved away from the dark entrance – someone was returning home. He was lucky as it was that no one had come earlier. He shuffled along slowly to the park. It was only a little way from here to the Stromovka. He sat down in the bushes. He would stay here for a few hours, alternately crouching, squatting and sitting, until he became too cold to stay any longer. November, he reflected, was not a suitable month for his attempts at saving himself, even if he was trying to save himself from something that was not altogether his own fault. Why did he get into this fix? The worst that could happen to a man was to be cast out from among the others. To be someone else than they. There was mankind, he thought, the poor, the poorest, the rich, the millionaires, the Jews and the others, Germans and Czechs, nations, castes, classes, groups, and then came he, Hynek Tausig, a nobody whom chance had pushed out of the ranks. He thought of the food queue there behind the fence, twisting and turning but all the people in it belonging together. Everyone belonged somewhere. Why had he not joined the transport immediately? It occurred to him that the simplest thing to do would be to walk into the police station near here or just hop into the river, as he was, all frozen through already. How long could it take? Or simply wait until a policeman came along through the park and stand up in front of him: here I am, officer. I'm not Alfred Janota, and I'm no Aryan either. I am Hynek Tausig, that's who. Would you do me a favour and put me among that crowd there behind the fence? Or take me with you. But if you would be so kind, I'd prefer the first, behind the fence. It won't mean a thing to you, you can just say you found me here and that I belong in this transport and not in the one that has gone. For you it means only a few steps and for me – just now it means everything that is called life.

But no policeman came along. Hynek Tausig felt his body going numb with the cold and prayed silently for the morning. When dawn came at last, he waited a little longer and then he straightened up with difficulty. His bones creaked. He parted the bushes and left the park. After a few hours of walking about in the streets he felt better. He was not alone in the streets. He decided to go and eat some hot soup. He was no longer so frightened as yesterday; he was near the fence. He ate his soup like a well-behaved boy, right down to the last spoonful. He would make it last until ten, then he would go again, and twice more during the day. Unless of course he managed in the meantime to get behind the fence! He licked the spoon. The man who invented buffets and off-the-ration watery soups was a fine fellow, he felt. He was helping him, lending him a hand in these ugly times when people were so terribly estranged from one another. No, he no longer experienced the terrors of yesterday. When one was tired, one probably became more indifferent to hardship, less aware of details, less frightened by everything. But perhaps that could be true the other way round, too.

Get in, only to get in. Get in, he told himself all the time. The very words urged him on to action. He heard some noises behind the fence. No, he could not climb it, that was certain. He must slip in with a new transport. He tapped his forehead with his forefinger. Why did he not think of that before! His eyes flashed with relief. And how about reporting directly at the Jewish congregation centre? It was from there, after all, that the call to the transport came. But what if the Gestapo had its people there too, what then? And even if not, they would hardly be delighted to see him since he had given them so much trouble – they had to get someone to go in his place when he did not turn up, did they not? No, he should not have risked the whole thing. Why did he do it, anyway? Was it meant as a defiant gesture? No, it was not that, a voice said inside him. But the fear he felt now was even worse. All right, he would not do it then. Still, he could do it the other way round – when those people came out from behind the fence, he would join them somehow.

He came to life. No more soup. He again felt the eagerness that had taken hold of him earlier. Something told him that this was well thought out. The dirty planks of the fence suddenly seemed lighter. Now to get a star.

A few minutes later chance sent him a man who could let him have one.

'Excuse me,' he stopped him, 'would you mind, a moment . . .'

The old man looked at him with black, searching eyes.

'What is it?' he asked.

c

His deliberately matter-of-fact voice was nevertheless slightly shaky. He was surprised, but at the same time a little relieved, by the unusual request. He was not wrong – the black-haired, ashen-looking little man in front of him did look as though he might have something to do with the Jews. He would hardly want the star as a souvenir. Though even that was possible. He had probably been out somewhere and was now returning home late. But what if he was a *provocateur*?

'What do you want it for?' he asked.

'I've lost mine,' Hynek Tausig replied. 'I'd get in trouble.'

No, no *provocateur* would manage to say it just like that. The old man unbuttoned his overcoat, tore the yellow star off his jacket, and handed it to him. Wait though, did he have a safety-pin on him as well? Yes, he had one all right, and he handed that to him too. 'And now good-bye, dear sir, we can't stand here like this for ever. You'd better go into the passage over there and pin it on.'

As Tausig did not do so, the old man walked away, looking back suspiciously over his shoulder until he reached the corner. Once there, he started to run, hurrying away, his breathing fast and laboured.

I am in luck after all, thought Hynek Tausig. This old gentleman was the first link in the chain of his good fortune. He walked on, almost happy. He had a yellow star in his pocket. He felt as if he were carrying, not a star, but a ton of dynamite, and gradually his tranquillity vanished. What if someone spoke to him? If they asked to see his identity card? How would he then explain that he had a Jewish star in his pocket?

He must not spoil anything. Coward! he swore at himself. Remembering the alcove, he thought how wonderful it was to be in the fresh air. Since the moment he had decided to join those behind the fence he was acting far more sensibly. Now the only thing that troubled him was hunger. But there was no time to eat. Again he stood by the entrance gate and the street was growing dark. He had the feeling that something was going on behind the fence. Today the noise had not ceased with the coming of night. Would they be coming out?

It was almost eleven. If they were taken out to the railway trucks this night, he would reach his destination. He thought of what was to come, and he trembled all over. The minutes became hours and hours an eternity. He waited until two. The noise did not cease. No, he would not return to the park, he would stay right here.

Through holes in the planks he saw the faint flicker of lights. Five past two. At last! The gates were thrown open and the first column came tumbling out. A hot wave flooded his whole body. His chin began to tremble. This is your moment, he told himself, go on! He left the shelter of the house wall, the yellow star in his pocket. He passed along the whole length of the small procession in order to find out who guarded them. And now a second column was coming out. About a hundred people. A single gendarme accompanied each group. Hynek Tausig quickly approached them. The gendarme shouted something. Was it meant for him? Of course it was – he was told to beat it or he would be taken along with the others! The gendarme chuckled; a good joke, that. 'All right, get along with you,' he said in a tone that was almost good-natured, 'before I change my mind!' This nation would make room for Germany anyway, he thought as he turned away from him. But these here were the first to go. Hynek Tausig, however did not hurry away. He would consider himself lucky if the gendarme really did it. So he went on in the same direction and at the same pace as before, only having veered slightly to the side. In one pocket he gripped the star, in another the safety-pin. Hurriedly he turned the corner and crossed the street to be on the opposite side of the road from the guard. It was now or never. With shaking hands he pinned the star to his coat. There, he said to himself, trying to summon up his courage which seemed to be ebbing all the time, now chuck the identity card into the sewer. The sewer grating grinned at him in the darkness a little way ahead. But he would not make it now, it was too late. The sound of steps. He stopped abruptly and quickly plucked the yellow cloth from his coat. With it he ripped off a piece of the garment. Good job he had his identity card in his hand – he could show it if necessary. But it was not necessary. The steps caught up with him and overtook him, a man's figure appeared in front of him and was quickly swallowed up in the darkness ahead. The column was drawing near. It began to snow. He turned up his collar and pinned the star on again to hide the rent in his coat. The gendarme was still at the head of the procession. Now – one quick jump, and he was in their midst. The people around him made a humming noise, then whispers could be heard. The gendarme turned round. 'Quiet there, or I'll knock your heads off!' Hynek Tausig pressed still closer to them, his eyes scanning the row he had joined. An old man, a married couple, two children. A family probably, it occurred to him. 'Give me that suitcase,' he whispered. The old man could not go on, he had dropped his hat and the column did not wait. 'Give me that suitcase,' Hynek Tausig repeated. 'I'll help you.' Then he added: 'I have to have something.' He did not even have the permitted fifty kilograms. 'Don't be afraid, give it to me,' he said, swearing and praying under his breath. 'Please lend me that bag, grandpa, for a while at least,' he murmured. If he had to go on like this another second, it would be too late. But the old man understood at last and passed him the suitcase. The gendarme appeared. 'No talking!' Who dared to disturb the silence – wasn't it enough for them that he had told them once already not to talk? 'Keep your bloody clappers shut!' he shouted. The woman could no longer carry her rucksack and her husband offered to help her. 'Quiet!' shouted the gendarme again, kicking the woman, whose suitcase dropped out of her hand and fell on the edge of the pavement. 'Hurry up, faster!' he yelled, and the column moved ahead at a slightly increased pace. It was snowing steadily. Hynek Tausig was taut with suspense for the gendarme was walking by his side.

Their eyes met. Hynek Tausig dropped his. How old could the boy be? Twenty. And he? A thousand by comparison. He contorted his mouth, on the point of blurting out that he begged for mercy, that he had done nothing wrong. After all, wasn't he where they wanted him? But the ashen-coloured face, the look on which made all this abundantly clear, was hidden by the night. The snow gleamed white in the darkness. They were now in a narrow street by the railway station. 'How many of you are there?' the gendarme shouted. So things were going to end badly in spite of everything, and so near his destination too. He might as well spill the truth. But before he could own up, before he forced himself to breach the barrier of silence caused by his cramped tongue, someone said, 'We didn't count the children.' Yes, that was quite likely, thought the gendarme, in the Reich only adults who were capable of work counted as people. 'All right, move along you pigs!' he called out. 'Move along!' To Hynek Tausig's ears this call meant salvation. Move along, you pigs, move along! The shout dissolved the rigidity of suspense within him and brought relief. Gone was the alcove and fear and the cramp of anxiety and the empty square. He was born anew this moment. Who was it who said the children had not been counted? He searched the dark throng, which slowly wended its way forward, for the man who had understood what was needed. The second link in the chain of his good fortune. Now he was one of the crowd. Move along, you pigs, move along! How nice it sounded when it applied to him as well.

Towards morning Hynek Tausig was loaded into the cattle truck. He was delirious with joy. He had been the eighty-fifth, the last to go in the truck. Full up! The truck was sealed and, together with thirty-seven others, sent off to Terezín.

The clanking noise of the bar on the outside of the truck's sliding door many hours later meant that they had reached their destination – the ghetto. Despite the fact that mere chance ordained that he should be one of the three who fell out of the overcrowded truck as soon as the door was opened by Jewish and German guards – and who were immediately slapped and kicked by Commandant Mönderling by way of welcome – he had the unassailable conviction that the third link in the chain of his good fortune had just been forged. The third and most important, he kept repeating to himself, or – as the saying went – third time lucky.

4

It was evening and he was going to bed. A very different evening from that on which he had felt his courage and resolution ebbing away. But he knew that tonight again he would not be able to sleep properly, for it would be the same as yesterday and tomorrow the same as a week ago. True enough, he woke early. He awoke with the picture of the town interwoven with a thousand threads in front of his eyes.

The ghetto looked emaciated at its star-point ends and swollen in the centre like the eruption of a volcano. In spite of the darkness he could feel life there, life in the shadow of death. The fortress resembled an overstuffed body. Through the single window in the ceiling he could see a darkly leaden sky. It looked as if it hung very low – in the early morning murk it seemed to be in danger of falling at any moment. It bit into the ground. Rain fell incessantly and heavy fog swirled round the ghetto gates.

At last it was five o'clock. He got up, dressed, went out. Outside, in front of the barracks, his pickaxe, painstakingly cleaned of every particle of dust, stood leaning against a tree. He picked it up and carried it towards the centre of the town.

He worked near the church, digging a well. By merely narrowing his eyes he no longer saw the earth. The same picture kept returning to him with dogged persistence: he was squatting in the Stromovka park, next to him a puddle. His puddle. He drank it dry, feeling the after-taste of dirt on his tongue. He spat. You are a coward, he reproached himself and went on digging the soft earth. Each time he struck with the pickaxe he re-lived it all once more, and again, over and over. Then he would console himself, thinking: what was I to do, everyone left me in the lurch. The earth was yielding

and clung to the steel. He busied himself with the cleaning of
the pickaxe.

Towards evening he put on his coat and returned to the
barracks.

The barracks he lived in were covered by tons of black,
soft earth. The cells were below the ground. Above and beside
the barracks towered the ramparts.

He lay down on his cot. He rolled about uneasily for a long
time, but again sleep would not come to him. It was not
dreams he was afraid of, he was afraid of morning. At long
last he fell asleep, a short, fitful sleep, the heavy, noisy breathing betraying the sleeper's disquiet. He was awakened by a
sharp whistle. The sound of a whistle did not frighten anyone,
it merely disturbed them. Yesterday the room orderly had
told them: 'There will be a muster tomorrow. I'll wake you
up at half past three, so see that you are all in the courtyard
by half past four.' He looked round him. Yes, that was it
now. He climbed out of bed. A muster, he grumbled, what the
hell's the use of that. But in his heart of hearts he was glad –
that hour between four and five was usually sleepless. He
put on his coat, glancing at the sewn-up rent on its front. He
went out. The overcoat, he thought vexedly, embodied everything. Even the incident with Oberscharführer Mönderling,
when he had all but kissed his arse in his gratitude that he had
been slapped and kicked for something totally different from
that which he had feared. This listless, taciturn forty-year-old
little man had forever been deprived of his peace of mind. The
others had all grown used to his taciturnity. He had nothing
to say about anything. He paid but scant attention even to the
war news. 'It'll all be over in six months, what d'you say, Mr
Tausig? Who knows, maybe it'll be next week already. But if
not earlier, then in six months for sure.' What was he to say?
He had heard all this a hundred times before. And it was
always 'for sure'. And yet, if he were not here, where would
he have gone? The room orderly was calling him. 'Don't you
go wandering off anywhere, Tausig. Wait here.' He was
responsible for having them all present and correct.

And so Hynek Tausig stood, looking up at the ramparts and farther still, at the darkness between the top of the wall and the rocks and the sky. It was going to rain again. After a while he pulled a piece of bread out of his pocket. He ate it slowly. He was one of a crowd. If they perished, he would perish with them. Nevertheless at the very bottom of his soul a vague discontent was stirring.

The night hovered long over the ghetto. Now at last its cloak began to be torn apart, the wind carrying shreds of darkness to the west. The rain started. But with it came the dawn. Hynek Tausig leaned his back against a tree and with a match started to pick his teeth, removing what had remained of the bread. Bread? It was no bread, but rather wood shavings, straw and bad flour with water. From inside the ghetto motley processions of people streamed towards the town gates. Crows circled above the ramparts, their croaking carrying towards the hills. Why do they sing to us, wondered Hynek Tausig, repeating their shrill cries to himself: craw, craw, craw.

'Where is your orderly?' he heard a voice behind him. 'We need a dozen men to tend the sick.'

Craw, craw. Why pick on me? he said to himself. He did not even turn round. Why must I swallow every bit of dirt which they want to slop at themselves in this wretched town?

'He's inside,' he said ungraciously. Then he pointed out to the man the strong digger who had made a writing desk of his narrow cot and was now ticking names off on his lists and counting them, unable to reach the required figure. And he was responsible for these people; if they should not all be here, Hynek Tausig told himself, he would be rewarded with a cell in the cellar of the *Kommandatur*, if not with a bullet. That was why they all had to be here, himself included, he told the messenger from the aged people's home, at the same time sending him to the devil in his mind.

After a lengthy argument, the room orderly agreed to release one man from his dormitory, if the gentleman would sign for him. As regards the others, let him kindly visit the other dormitories. 'Who is finished?' he asked. Someone told him. Hynek Tausig. 'He's outside in the courtyard.' Thank you, the messenger knew that himself.

Thus it was that Hynek Tausig became a male nurse for the day, a day which had held out the promise of a rest from his pickaxe.

They walked side by side without saying a word.

The streets of Terezín intersected the ghetto with the monotony common to all garrison towns. 'Well, here we are,' said the messenger suddenly. 'When you're finished you can go back to your people.' With that he left, full of unspoken anxiety that he would not be able to fulfil his mission satisfactorily. But, thought Hynek Tausig, he is probably glad he can go around looking for people to do the job and does not have to lend a hand himself. The thought was immediately followed by the objection that finding people for the job was difficult enough, but he did not turn to look after him.

The house he had just entered was ornamented by three stone bears. He had no need to ask anyone anything. People with sticks and crutches in their hands were carrying down the stairs those of their fellow inmates for whom such aids were no longer enough. Someone was weeping and holding on to the banisters, refusing to vacate the stairs. There were loud cries. 'They're killing us!' Hynek Tausig turned that way, but somebody behind him shouted in his ear: 'Why don't they do it here?' That's true, he thought. He wanted to turn in the direction of the voice when he heard an unpleasant female contralto crying out in the courtyard: 'A cart was to be sent for me!'

He did not report to anyone. He simply took his coat off and began to carry the old people down the stairs. His face assumed an ashen colour, the moustache which sprouted on it having a queer hue, neither black nor grey. His hair, too, which kept falling across his forehead, was no longer dark black, but had taken on the ash-grey tint of bird's feathers.

At last they were all downstairs.

Two corpses, shrouded in white sheets, lay by the wall in

the courtyard, away from the others. Hynek Tausig's gaze was impelled in their direction. People die, he thought, and have their children about them. When you are eighty you know that you have not much longer to live. You wait for the end and are not afraid of what is between heaven and earth. Here it was all different. You were all alone when you died. Perhaps these two were both still alive when he carried them down a while ago. Now it was all over for them.

He strolled leisurely out into the street. Turning round, he caught sight of the animals carved in the stone above the entrance.

Should he go back to the barracks? He felt neither a duty to return, nor any compassion for the old men. He was like the stone bears who would be the dead men's only mourners. In the end, however, he came to the conclusion he would do best to go along with the old men. He would help them keep together.

They walked out of the entrance, taking with them the two corpses. They had been told that all of them were required to come out for the muster to be taken.

They trooped out of the house. The muster was to take place on the Common – there was not enough room for all of them anywhere else. But surely it could have been done in the houses and in the streets, reflected Hynek Tausig. To weigh, count, and write down everybody and everything. It would have been like one immense stock-taking. So many people, so many pairs of shoes, hats, laces, and rings. All of a sudden he realized he had parted from those he had wanted to help. He started to push one of the carts which collected the dead every morning and brought the bread every noon. The face of the man limping next to him seemed familiar to him. He racked his brain, wondering who it could be. Was it not the old man whom he helped with his suitcase that night he joined the transport? Was it – or wasn't it? It occurred to him suddenly, as he scanned the faces of all those near him, that they were all exactly the same.

Someone was choking on the highway. He did not turn

round. But he should. Certainly he should. All right, he would do it, then. But by this time the sick person was sitting down on the kerb and someone was bending over him, hiding his face from view. I am always late for everything, Hynek Tausig thought. He let go of the cart. Better look out for himself. But it was unpleasant to walk along empty-handed, pushed and jostled by the crowd. That conductor on the tram, he recalled, he had helped him too. He had not asked for his help, and it was doubly nice of him that he helped without being asked. One did not forget such things. He did not even know him. It was hardly likely they would ever meet again. What was he doing – if he was still alive? Lost in his thoughts of the conductor, he glanced involuntarily at another cart, on which there were women. 'Water, water!' He raised his eyes and said: 'You'll have to wait until we get to the Common. There's no water here.' Then, in a louder voice, he asked: 'Anybody got anything to drink?' Someone handed him a bottle, which he held up to the sick woman's lips. She drank and repaid him with a grateful smile. He felt he did not deserve it – after all, he had only acted as a mediator. But the look he had received had been worth it. 'Whose is the water?' he asked in a husky voice. 'Leave it to those people,' he heard the reply. No, it occurred to him, people did not always behave like beasts. And he thought of himself. Not always. He pushed the cart, repeating to himself: 'It's true, people don't always behave like beasts.' He put his shoulder to the cart and pushed.

It was almost eleven in the morning when they reached the Common.

Hynek Tausig stood in the middle, looking round at the great obedient mass of people. He reproached himself. Why had he, in spite of all his cowardice, not been rendered sufficiently apathetic by all he had seen so far to be able to bear it with indifference? A horse gets a lash of the whip if he does not pull properly, he mused, but a human being does not forget the blows. They still smarted even though the bruise had long disappeared. And it was all the worse for that.

An imperceptible flurry ran through the crowd. He could feel it too. At last he decided to ask. What was happening? Every tenth? He raised his head in surprise. What did that mean? Then someone said it full out, in a whisper: 'Every tenth will go to the wall.' 'Why?' 'No particular reason.' They said someone was missing. There would be hell to pay. Every tenth, that might be me, Hynek Tausig admitted to himself. But, he added quickly, you can just as well be every fifth or every second. What a fine sight it would be if all the sixty thousand people here on the Common started to run, he thought. They could hardly hope to catch them. But nobody ran. So that was it: every tenth. No trouble, everything nice and quiet. First, second, third – and tenth! Fall out! Nothing for it, he reflected, startled; he would have to fall out. One had sometimes to do it, willynilly. Neighbours embraced each other. He had nobody to embrace him. He stood there, a queer, emaciated little man. No wife, no children – come to think of it, he would find it easier to bear than someone for whom the number ten will mean splitting his family. This, then, was also life, these moments of waiting whether one would be the tenth.

He did not know how long he had been standing there when he heard the SS say: 'You on the outside, count off in hundreds. Form columns and divide them off two paces from one another.' No more talk of shooting. So it was not true.

He looked up at the sky. From somewhere up there came the roar of a plane. The sky had grown blue and light, perhaps it was beautiful. Man, he reflected, is the king of all creation. He can fly higher than the birds, but he can also fall lower than any other living thing. And again he thought of himself. 'Down!' he heard them cry. Why, he wondered. The crowd rumbled, then he heard the whispers: 'That's the end, they're going to bomb us!' As if nothing of this concerned him. Hynek Tausig watched all of them lying down, the entire sixty-thousand-strong mass. Unhurriedly he turned and saw a group of people praying, others kissing each other. His eyes returned to the sky. Should he get down, too? But he did not lie down. Now he was the only one standing up. Someone pulled at his trouser leg. He was seized by a sudden impulse to kick the unknown man in the face. The plane had passed. Perhaps it would come back, it occurred to Hynek Tausig, and would drop its bombs. But it did not concern him. Had he then fallen out of the ranks? That frightened him – he must stick with the crowd, otherwise he'd again get into trouble as that other time. But the fear shown by the crowd was repulsive to him. He went on standing. I lack the courage to lie down, he told himself. And when he saw the others getting up from the ground, he did not feel any better. He was pleased neither by having refrained from lying down, nor by having remained standing.

Thus it happened that he was the first to see the ghetto commandant, Fritz Mönderling, as he came riding towards them on horseback. Spick and span in his best uniform, he made for the only point of orientation on the Common, greyish-black with its crowd of human bodies. And that point was he, Hynek Tausig.

The SS got busy. They had whips and rifles – in a few moments sixty thousand people were standing in ragged groups of a hundred each. The groups made way for the rider.

Now the commandant was right in the middle.

Up to this moment Hynek Tausig watched the ghetto elder pushing towards him, almost simultaneously with the rider on horseback. The elder bore a resemblance to him, to Tausig. The strongest among his mixed feelings was curiosity: what was to happen now?

At last the elder arrived.

'The count today, Herr Commandant,' he reported, hoarse and out of breath, 'is fifty-nine thousand, nine hundred and eighty-seven swinish Jews.'

It looked as if he were reporting to the horse, his eyes being on a level with the horse's mouth. It's like in school, it occurred to Hynek Tausig. Quite a bright pupil, knows the answer pat.

'People missing?' the commandant interrupted the report.

The insignificant man in front of the horse had once been a lecturer at Frankfurt University. He was silent. He had done something wrong and would be caned in front of the class.

'You'll take the consequences!' barked the man on horse-back. Then he rode off through the gap which had been formed on his arrival and had remained politely open.

The SS men were shouting. The ghetto was pouring back behind the fortress ramparts. Hynek Tausig was engulfed by the crowd. Was that all? he wondered. Everyone was walking on his own, but he would again push. Those in front had already reached the ghetto gates. He felt that something had been born within him that gave him the sensation of having returned. Yet nothing extraordinary was going on – the hovels were merely being filled up again. The town between the ramparts was being filled, filled in the same way as useless junk was stuffed into the dustbin. Was that a return? Yes, it was: he, too, was a piece of junk.

Next morning he again rolled uneasily on his cot. But this time it had begun already at half past three. That was a fine thing, on top of everything else. He asked himself a strange question. Why do your actions, Hynek Tausig, not correspond to that which every human being, yourself included, longs for? Not to resemble a mouse seeking a way out of the trap. But all of life, he contradicted himself, resembles a cat, a mouse, and a trap. And he – he was only a mouse, a small, lonely and frightened mouse. Did he, though, really long for anything else? Was he not, if the truth were known, glad that he was what he was?

By the time he got up to collect his pickaxe and go off to dig the well outside the church he was more tired and worn than he would be in the evening, after twelve uninterrupted hours of digging, despite the fact that he was a thin, gaunt little man not weighing more than fifty-five kilograms.

Yes, that was what he was, a mouse; a mouse that was scared to death by the thought of a cat in its vicinity – or at least a trap.

5

He walked across the ghetto.

He had grown still leaner. His roaming eyes had sunk deep and they had an unpleasant, expectant gleam. They resembled a membrane. He had learned to register the slightest vibrations and pulsations of the town. It had become a subconscious process that went on incessantly. Yes, something was happening. Be careful, Hynek Tausig, he commanded himself. Something was in the air.

At ten in the morning the car from the German *Kommand-atur* drove up to the house of the Council of Elders. Nobody was any longer in doubt as to what was in preparation. A transport. Invisible mouths passed the information on to sixty thousand ears.

The information reached him too. He gave a start, but then he thought perhaps he would not be in it. Another piece of news: 'Half the ghetto is to go.' Why should he, of all people, be left out? He had no one here who would remove his card from the index of the records department, according to which the transport was to be compiled. And even if he had – would that alter anything if half the ghetto was to be sent away? He had long felt hostility towards the big fortress. He had an antipathy to this town, did not like the stone beak, bent six times, which pecked at the streets and houses, and which let people see that they used to look different. He had lost the sensation of having returned, that relaxing satisfaction he had felt when Mönderling had beaten him, and again when the muster was over.

He walked between the ramparts, from one corner to the other. The well outside the church was finished and he was now working on the railway line, on the Terezín-Bohušovice track. When you have finished the railway line, he told himself, you will ride on it to Poland. Why did he not go back to the barracks and sleep? He had spent the whole night remov-

ing the last projecting rock with a pneumatic drill. What was it
he was looking for anyway?

The ghetto was narrow, but you could not traverse it from
end to end even in four hours. Now he had reached the
Kavalír barracks. Nothing about them was in keeping with the
noble name. Inside, behind the bars, were mental patients.
Someone in there was just raising his right arm in the Nazi
salute. A nurse came running and took him away to a cell.
Something forced Hynek Tausig to give a nasty laugh. What
was the difference between that woman and the lunatic, he
reflected. She drew attention to herself even more than he did.
Whose attention, though, came the disappointing thought.
Theirs – the Jews. What did it matter to him, Hynek Tausig?
He pressed his forehead against the cool bars. He did not feel
like going to the barracks. In his heart of hearts he knew why.
He was afraid that on his cot he would find a card with the
summons to join the transport. But let him not think about
that. He reached the sappers' barracks which had been turned
into a hospital. Hospital? Was it not funny, to heal people so
that they would be able to go with the transport? In the yard
next to the barracks he could see old men praying. They
were leaning against the latrine wall, white papers and black
prayer books in their hands. The rabbis had come to the conclusion that the ghetto was a stone preserve. If nothing else,
they thought, ancient religious customs would at least be
maintained here. But the preserve was to become a museum,
reflected Hynek Tausig. Nothing living would remain here.

He walked faster. Again that unseen whip cracking in his
ears. Transport. And somewhere in the background bigger
doses of beating. And then the end. A very different end to
that which the boys were in the habit of conjuring up after
returning from work – according to which a neighbour would
one day turn up, saying: 'Go on, run along home, you idiots,
the war is over.' The hope of this kind of end slumbered on in
them in spite of everything, despite the fact that they post-
poned the date of Germany's defeat from day to day and from
year to year. The hope lived in him, too, even in moments

when he was not actually thinking of it, yes even when he deliberately tried to avoid it in his thoughts. In spite of it all he was encouraged by this faint, indistinct mirage. Somewhere something was waiting. And now it was to be spoiled.

The nearer he came to the barracks, the greater his fear that he would be among those included in the transport. He was again hurrying with his head bent forward. You have been like this before, Hynek Tausig, in Prague, on your way between the alcove and Wenceslas Square – should he not stop and straighten up? But he did not slacken speed and he did not turn round. The corners of his narrow mouth drooped. His face was a dark ashen colour, distorted by a wild grimace. Suddenly he stopped, as though he had run up against an invisible wall. Why was he rushing so? In order to hold the summons card in his hand twenty seconds earlier? He was almost certain that the white card lay on his cot. But how could he be certain, was he clairvoyant or what? Why cross his bridges before he came to them? He understood then that if man was ever in his life a beast, then it was fear that made him so. Why was he standing here foolishly like this? He realized that he was standing still and people were treading on his toes. Yes, it was fear that did it, every child knew that. Only he did not know it, not he. He started walking again. He was afraid that he would be included in the transport, was he not? But he had been through this before. Nevertheless, in spite of the knowledge he had just gained, fear again predominated. He could only think of the transport, and whether he would be in it. Something told him it was different, but a second voice said, no it wasn't, it was the same. He too. One did not change at forty-one. He had remained the same. A coward, he added in disgust. He had been born only to tremble for his mousy little life.

In the faces of the passers-by he saw himself. All of them were cowards, once and for all, he consoled himself, not only he. They trembled for their own sake and concealed it by pretending to be afraid for someone else. But then he thought

D

that even if he did get left out of it, he would go and beg to be taken along.

He was in front of the barracks. He entered, full of the reserve and excitement of fear. His cot . . . his cot was empty. He felt better. Oh yes, the life of a mouse, but at least it was not over yet. He was not going. He sank wearily on to the cot.

'When did they come with the cards?' he asked the room orderly.

'As soon as you left.'

'And what about you?'

'Not me, but my mother is in it.'

He nodded, but felt at the same time that this gesture lacked true sympathy. The orderly was thirty. He had been digging on various building sites since the 'AK' transport, which had been the first to arrive here and had had most of the hard work. So his mother was going. They would be separated. No, nothing stayed together in this place. At home it was all different, a mother was everything, she had respect, and a quiet old age. Not so here. The mother would go and the son would be glad he had been left behind. In a week's time he would go with another transport and would reproach himself that each of them had gone off to die on his own.

'Mother is seventy,' said the digger. 'I shan't let her go alone. I'm going to report with her.'

I am a swine, Hynek Tausig said to himself. That is how things are: some men are human beings and some are beasts. And some a little of both, and that's me. But most of all I am a swine.

'I guess you're doing the right thing,' he said quietly, adding: 'I'd do the same myself.' This time he was quite sure he really would. This time he was not lying. Still, he was glad he did not have to do it, and he went out again.

It was evening. He returned to the room, which was different from yesterday. It looked like a military camp. The boys were packing their stuff. The gloom of the first moments had gone. His eyes lighted on the digger and he went over to help him. Then he helped his neighbour. He did not say a word the whole time. Finished.

'Lights out, chaps,' the digger called out when they had all finished.

Time to sleep.

But Hynek Tausig could not sleep. He kept thinking that there were a great many things in a human being, something of the beast too, but that it was up to him to choose; maybe nobody was going to ask him about it after the war. Perhaps he would not have to answer the question: were you in a blue funk, old fellow, or did you not give a damn? After the war, if only he lived to see it, life would be completely different. No one would need to know anything, either about himself or anyone else. One could live without that, just as one did before. Everything would be plain sailing. Good morning and good-bye. Without being kicked and called names. No, he had never imagined that he would carry out a revolution in his life. It was not to be recommended at his age.

Sleep stayed away from him as the night advanced. Bitter thoughts pinned him down on his cot. He could smell the pungent odour of human bodies. He was sure not to sleep any more now. Well then, Hynek Tausig, you are going to live through it all, obedient as ever, helping your pals to the trucks. And if by chance you should stumble under someone's foot, or even into one of the trucks, you will not say a word. No, he would not sleep now, but just lying there was also difficult. He got up, put on his coat, and went to the door. He was not allowed out, but he could look out of the door, could he not?

It was a clear night. The silky blue of the sky was illuminated by the glow of immensely distant diamonds. When you were small, Hynek Tausig, you thought everything was like the stars, pure and beautiful. What would become of man? He could not tear himself away. He stood there for hours, hours and minutes.

The transport left in the morning.

The ashen-looking little man did not move from his place.

Evening came again, and with it night. He would not go to bed. He would remain there, by the door. Today it would be different.

The ghetto lay at his feet. A strange prison, he thought sleepily. Every part of a man was imprisoned separately, broken in pieces. One transport had left. There now remained an invisible time limit for the next. When that ran out, it would all begin anew.

Someone was calling to him: 'Don't stand there gaping, man! You'll be as weak as a fly in the morning.'

He felt a sudden chill and pulled his coat more closely around him. He forgot to reply.

A moment later he came back to his cot and bent down to look under it. There he had the suitcase he had borrowed. He tore away the paper and pulled out Alfred Janota's identity card. It seemed to him all of a sudden that a man of that name really lived somewhere. He had to find him and give him his life.

Slowly he pushed the identity card into his pocket. He still had some money left. The world seemed huge and free to him now. But that was a deceptive impression, everyone had to find himself a narrow little street. A street of his own. And to walk that street and not turn left or right. Once you did that, you would not be able to go straight again. He could not go to the north-west, where the mountains were. What about the south? No, he must not start doubting, otherwise he would never do it. He went to the door, feeling the snores, the sweaty odours and the breathed-up air behind his back. He stood there, looking at the sky. The clouds were thick and dark and there were no stars.

A look at his watch. A little after twelve. He looked back at the room he was leaving. They were all asleep now. Should he perhaps stay? He might not be in the next transport either. He was safely hidden in a crowd. He must not behave reck- lessly . . . the echo of the last word did not have time to reverberate through him. No, he must not stop now. He must not undress and get back in bed like a cowardly mouse. By morning he could walk at least twenty kilometres. But if he went to bed now, he would be stronger tomorrow. Take it easy, he admonished himself, take it easy. And don't try to fool yourself! His chin trembled. They might catch him. But wasn't he as good as caught now, this very minute that he was thinking it? That was how it was that time in Prague. He need not look for a gap in the fence. Why not climb into some empty truck at the station and let himself be taken away, far from the ghetto. And then – no, he must not lie to himself.

He stood there a moment longer. Then he left the doorway. But not to return inside.

A little later, concealed by the night, Hynek Tausig stopped on the northern rampart of the ghetto. He caught hold of the bough of a tall cherry tree whose thin trunk grew less than a yard away from the reddish slopes of the ramparts. He clambered down rather clumsily – he was afraid and that hampered him. He scratched his face and hands and coat on the bark of the tree, but at last he felt the damp yielding earth beneath his feet. He glanced up, murmuring to himself: 'I'm leaving.' It sounded inside him, however, as if he were trying to convince himself.

And then, slightly bent forward, he ran through the night and the mud, past the gendarmes' post.

Rose Street

I

THE breath of summer blew through the ghetto.

It carried Elizabeth Feiner, known for short as 'Auntie', right up to the junk shop on L Avenue. The street, as you could see by looking at the street-sign on the corner by the barracks, used to be called Rose Street – it had not been an avenue, nor had this town been a ghetto, while the barber's shop, 'The Sun', closed down long before the war, could hardly have served for the sale of junk and cast-offs.

The Star Fort was being smartened up. The German H.Q. building, where they were expecting a visit from Switzerland, had been whitewashed to resemble the other houses in the ghetto, beneath the scaffolding old women were scrubbing the pavement, and real roses appeared in the earth around the stone fountains.

There were no glass panes in the once wooden door of the shop, and Elizabeth Feiner had covered up the holes with greasy, brownish paper that looked like stretched donkey skin. From the dark interior of the shop she could watch the shadows and the heads flitting past. That was all she saw.

Ever since that morning, which had been hot and stifling, she announced to all comers that she had nothing really worthwhile in stock. Her slightly rasping voice, in which kindness mingled with irritation, suggested that the junk shop of which she was in charge through no wish of her own, was no less a fake than the roses and the ostentatious L Avenue.

When the door of the shop opened, the old woman's ugly head dropped down almost on to her chest.

'Good morning, Mrs Feiner.' The words came through the rustle of paper.

The door creaked twice.

The man who came in, ceremoniously taking off his hat, worn even now in summer low on his forehead, slowly placed two boiled potatoes on the counter.

'Perhaps you can use them,' he said.

'Oh, Mr Spiegel,' protested Elizabeth Feiner. 'What have I done to deserve this?'

Embarrassed, the old man closed his eyes hesitantly. 'My dear Mrs Feiner,' he said, 'that's a question we might all ask. But whom?'

His lips, once fleshy, were now coagulated by the bronze-purplish coating of anaemia into small, whitish clots of a boyishly gentle smile.

'You are incorrigible,' said Elizabeth Feiner.

'I suppose I am,' nodded the old man.

She would have liked to stroke his veiny hand. But she only asked almost absent-mindedly: 'Do you need anything?'

'No, thank you.'

He was ashamed of his husky voice. He must go at once – he had only wanted to look in, anyway.

'Well, I'd better be going.'

'Good-bye, Mr Spiegel.'

The familiar creak of the door, and the bent back disappeared behind the greasy paper. Silence. Elizabeth Feiner mutely substituted other, far more friendly, words for the echo of the greeting, wishing herself au revoir soon, as she did every time Joachim Spiegel came, though at the same time she doubted it. How cleverly he passed from the small things to the big ones which she did not understand, she thought to herself.

The shadows were now more sharply outlined. The sun was sailing through a pink sea towards the other side of the town. As soon as it crossed over the beige gable of the house opposite, it would be noon. When it disappeared behind the rock with the eagle beak, the day would be over. If only the sun were more friendly, Elizabeth Feiner thought, it would stay longer in the sky. Or it would sail faster. But anyway, who knew which would be better?

She opened the ledger. She had sold nothing today. But even nothing must be entered, for the Reich was great and strict. It occurred to her that if a thousand Elizabeths decided to mess up their accounts, the war could hardly last so long. Then, however, she waved the thought away with her hand. Nonsense. She pushed aside the potatoes, which to her personified the image of the kind, old man, and picked up a blue-and-white pencil.

Nevertheless, she noticed that the greasy paper on the door was again darkened. The door flew open as someone kicked it – she could hear the sharp, dry sound of the kick – from the outside. The paper was torn off and fell slowly into the street. The shop was flooded with light, and she saw the greenish-grey uniform and reddish face of an officer.

He came bursting into the room, shouting: 'You bloody old Jewish whore!'

Two long strides and he was in front of her and slapped her face.

Werner Binde, the driver from H.Q. waddled in with his rolling gait.

It seemed for the moment as if by slapping her the officer had given vent to all that raged inside him, as if now he was at a loss what to do and what to say. His eyes travelled around the little shop, until at last they rested on the wooden, shiny top of the counter.

'The account books!' he gritted through his teeth.

He had decided it would be undignified to let the old Jewess witness – however shortly – the indecision of a German officer.

Elizabeth Feiner was, however, aware only of his menacing stare.

'Where's your husband?' he asked suddenly.

'He died,' she said.

'How's that?'

She shrugged.

That was too much for Herz.

'Get into the corner!' he roared.

She was so frightened that she failed to do as she was bid. She had not the slightest idea why she had been singled out for this visit; she could not know that at approximately the same time when she was deliberating whether Joachim Spiegel could become her partner in her old age and death, Herz had been called to see the newly-appointed commandant of the town, Albert Ritsche. Somebody had reported to him that they had seen someone in the ghetto smoking. What had the First Officer to say to that?

'Into the corner with you, Jewish swine!' shouted Herz, irritated by her apathy. 'At once, and be quick about it!'

Werner Binde was looking on with the same cold interest with which he had earlier scanned the shelves on the walls of the shop. If Herz had not told him outright to follow him, he would quite probably have stayed behind in the car. He transferred his weight from one foot to the other, rocking nonchalantly on his heels. Ever since the old commandant, Wolf Seidl, had left and the new one arrived without Berlin having appointed anyone of those who had served here longer, the H.Q. resembled a stirred up wasps' nest, with everyone manœuvring for the best positions. Old sympathies had been disrupted and the officers were in no hurry to establish new ones. They were waiting to see what Ritsche was like. And Binde had only a while ago heard him telling Herz off. The old woman, whom Herz had picked on to work off his rage, repelled Binde by her ugliness. If not she, he thought, someone else would have copped it instead. Nothing of this showed on Binde's face, however. On the contrary, it looked rather as if he was merely dividing up the shoddy things on the shelves in his mind, choosing the ones he had a use for and discarding those he did not want.

Herz turned to him suddenly, taking him by surprise, but Binde retained his composure. He brought his heels together with a loud click and said the first thing that came to his mind: 'There's no water in the tank, sir. Shall I go and fetch some?'

'No, stay here,' said Herz, adding sybilantly, 'Ass!'

It did not occur to him in the least that he was being unjust, having told Binde earlier that he would not need the car any more today. Nor did it occur to Binde himself, or so it seemed by the look in his cool, unconcerned, fish-like eyes.

Then Herz turned again to Elizabeth Feiner. Raising his hand, he made a threatening gesture right under her nose, the taut skin of his grey buckskin glove emphasizing the outlines of his clenched fist.

What a revolting hook of a nose, he thought with distaste, and said: 'We'll soon knock rebellion out of your heads. As for you, you scab, you'll get a taste of it right here and now.'

All her astonishment was written large in her wrinkled, sinewy and angular face and in the eyes with which she gazed on him. Why had they come here, of all places?

'Don't play the innocent with me,' said Herz, as though he had read her thoughts.

'But I really don't know, sir . . .' she said.

'Shut up,' Werner Binde hissed at her from the other side of the shop.

Elizabeth Feiner was, however, already sorry she had spoken.

Herz suddenly changed his tone. 'Sarah, dear, don't you think your takings are very small?' he said, his voice sweet and coaxing.

And Werner Binde looked on as Herz pulled out of his well-polished black jackboot a length of reed, at whose end there was a dully gleaming lead pellet, doing it slowly and almost imperceptibly, so that the old woman should not see.

Elizabeth Feiner was still standing motionless in a corner of the shop underneath the clergymen's chasubles and the gloomy black-and-white folds of stoles which hung from a round, wooden rod. Every now and then they would swing to and fro as they were touched by the wind or by the breath of the two men, and she would feel them quite close to her face. She closed her eyes and breathed in their pungent naphthalene smell. But she did not dare to raise her hand and push them aside.

'Come here!' the officer called out to her.

She came back slowly, leaving the surplices to flutter behind her.

'Turn round,' said Herz.

Elizabeth Feiner, her chin dropping timorously on to her chest, cast an uncertain glance at Herz's purplish face, at the root of his red nose, and at the cold eyes of Werner Binde, in whose depths she thought she saw a glimmer of mute disagreement.

Binde was leaning against the shelf and examining the old clothes. No, he could not use any of this stuff, his mouth with its slightly raised left corner seemed to indicate. But these sparks went out very quickly. Herz had taken off his cap and was hanging it up with exaggerated care on the peg. The inevitable was about to begin, and Binde's eyes went cold again as before.

Herz prodded Elizabeth Feiner with his elbow. Beneath the surface of his rage there was a gap of tranquillity. And in this gap he found both the impulse and the explanation of what he had come to do, which showed so vividly on his face that Elizabeth Feiner shuddered in fear of her life. For the eyes into which she was gazing and the face which was now frozen in a chilly immobility were the living image of death.

Herz drew his arm back in abhorrence. The figure in front of him was no woman – it was the incarnation of Ritsche's reproof. He was faced with the task of obliterating that which had besmirched his soldierly honour.

He did not speak another word; but when the dirty, old Jewish swine collapsed on to the counter at a single shove, as he had wished her to do, he could not help guffawing aloud with merriment.

Binde made no remark now, though he knew well enough that politeness demanded that he should. His mind was pre-occupied with the thought that the events of this afternoon were like skittles, knocking each other down although only one of them had been hit by the bowl. That conceited mug, Herz, had told him off because it had occurred to him to say that he had no water in the tank, yet he could just as easily have said he had no petrol, only because he had himself been given a dressing down earlier. Why? Because someone in this damned town had smoked, or perhaps even no one had smoked at all. Perhaps someone only imagined it. And now this old woman, whose days were numbered in any case, was going to pay for it. In the silence that followed Herz's laugh, Binde realized that if he now let Herz go through with this act without lending a hand, Herz would be sure to ram it down his throat at the most inopportune moment. He therefore responded with a belated, sour grin.

But the corners of Herz's mouth were by this time only imperceptibly curved. The surface of his mood had risen in a tempestuous wave, which completely flooded the tranquil gap. The spark which had kindled his smile had now flared up into action.

Herz kicked the motionless feet, shod in old-fashioned goloshes with buckles. It came to his mind that this was not Russia; these bastards obligingly waited until one chose to kick them.

Elizabeth Feiner lay slumped over the wooden counter, the blunt edge of which pressed against her stomach. Her eyes were closed. She could feel all the time how the blood streamed to her head; but it was no longer a head – it was a barrel which seemed to be bursting and yet was completely empty. There was a swoon inside that barrel, and it would claim her as soon as she gave it enough blood. Even thus, with her eyes closed, she saw Joachim Spiegel; he came again and brought her potatoes. Then she had an incredibly silly idea – it occurred to her that all three, the entire phantom of a funeral procession, Joachim Spiegel and both the soldiers who had come in, were from one and the same country. Who would have thought it a little while ago. Lucky they did not notice the potatoes – after all, they were not merely pieces of starch

with a few vitamins in them, they secreted within themselves
kindness and self-sacrifice. All these thoughts, which took
place almost at the very ceiling of her consciousness, rapidly
succumbing to a swoon, were responsible for her being able to
feel nothing but the blows. It was only when the officer lost
his head and started to beat her in a way calculated to make
her cry out that she gave up all thought. By that time she was
so far gone that she did not utter a sound.

It was half-past five, and Herz replaced his whip in his boot.
She had got hers all right, even though she didn't make a noise,
he thought, looking at the old woman's back.

'Well, Binde, what d'you say?' he asked in a voice of tired
satisfaction as he took off his gloves. 'Neat work, wasn't it?'

'Very neat, sir . . .' said Binde.

Herz pushed the door open with a vigorous movement and
stood on the threshold. Proudly, with a bluishly purple face,
bloodshot and covered with sweat, he looked up and down L
Avenue. Today, he thought, his pride swelling still further,
today they'll be talking about me all over the ghetto.

Werner Binde followed him out of the shop.

But Elizabeth Feiner did not yet know that she was alone.

She lay across the counter in such a way that she could not
fall off. She swallowed her tears, and only then did she manage
to faint.

2

'It's gone half-past five, Binde,' Herz said when they were
back in the car. 'Tomorrow's another day.'

'Do you wish to go back to H.Q., sir, or shall I drive you
home?' asked Binde.

'Don't you like boxing?' asked Herz, following a different
line of thought. He was no longer thinking of the old woman.
And it occurred to him that there had been in the family, on
his mother's side, an uncle Helmuth Rinde or Binde or some
such name. He felt wonderful. Then he added, 'Home.'

The driver nodded. Did he like boxing? That, after all, was not boxing. It was a thrashing, and a pretty mean one at that. All right, he thought, they'd put all Jews on the same garbage heap. Well, let them rot there then, but by themselves.

'Do you know something, Binde?' Herz asked him gaily. 'Perhaps we are relatives.'

Binde saw that Herz's foul mood had been left behind in the town, where he had shaken off the load of abuse piled on him by the new commandant.

'How come?' he asked. 'Your name is Herz and mine Binde, you come from Hamburg and I from Berlin.'

'Are you free this evening?' Herz began, again on another tack.

'I guess so,' replied Binde.

'Come and have dinner with us,' said Herz, his voice filled with satisfaction, for he had no doubt that the commandant would find out from the Jewish elder's report how he had dealt with that Jewess.

'Thanks,' said Binde.

There was nothing in this reply, however, to tell Herz whether Binde had accepted the invitation or not.

Werner Binde stared with cold eyes at the road ahead, conscious at the same time of Herz's searching gaze upon him. They had once driven together to Berlin like this, at a time when Herz was deputizing for Wolf Seidl. Herz told him, laughingly, that his eyes reminded him of a fish. That was the first time he had taken a dislike to Herz. He really did sometimes concentrate so intently on something that it seemed as though all activity had ceased behind that blunt, low brow of his. And now there was an unexpected invitation inside the limited circle of Werner Binde's cumbrous thought.

Herz stared at Binde's mask-like profile. He had been glad at the time that he had been allotted Binde, the best driver at H.Q. It was something in the nature of a distinction. Binde was not over-popular – they nicknamed him 'kohlrabi' because of his low, foreshortened head – but he was not unpopular, either. His Army papers said that his reliable driving had

served SS General Erich von Stumpke in the Buchenwald concentration camp, and later the head of the Reich Winterhilfe
for South Germany, Oswald Trautenfelder. He had been
transferred from Buchenwald at his own request, which fact,
Herz recalled, had at first given rise to all sorts of conjectures.
Nevertheless it was possible, and Herz was inclined to take
that view himself now, that it had all been a personal matter.
Still, there was something slightly fishy about the chap. They'd
discussed it with Ritsche when he took up his post, but he had
only said:

'One camp or another, what's the difference?'

And the conjectures had ceased.

A little later Binde stopped the car in front of a yellow villa.
Herz's wife, Rosemarie Ilse, a stoutish woman of thirty-five
with a white skin, light blue, watery eyes, and a head that sat
upon her fat shoulders as though she had no neck, was waiting by the gate in front of the garden.

'Maurice,' she called out. 'At last you're home! Oh, Herr
Binde . . . your name is Binde, isn't it?'

The driver nodded.

'You must be tired,' Rosemarie Ilse went on. 'Come on in,
both of you.'

The eight-year-old Adolf barred their way as they entered
the gate.

'Heil Hitler!' he shouted at his father.

Herz stroked his head, but the little boy drew away,
offended.

'I said Heil Hitler, daddy, and you didn't.'

'Well, all right then, "Heil Hitler" . . .'

Little Adolf, however, burst into tears.

'Binde will have dinner with us tonight,' said Herz.

That, of course, was more than Rosemarie Ilse had reckoned
with. Since when was Maurice inviting non-coms. to his
house? She had intended to offer Binde a glass of something –
after all, he was also a German, and she knew well enough
that they had to stick together in this hostile land. But dinner?

She stared at her husband in surprise, but a single grimace on his reddish face sufficed to keep her quiet.

Binde did not notice anything. So they were perhaps relatives. What was he to think of that?

They sat down in the drawing-room.

Herz's five-year-old daughter came running up to him. She was better behaved than her brother and had waited for her father here. She was called Rosemarie after her mother and grandmother, and Hilde after the mother-in-law.

'Did you annoy mother today?' asked Herz.

Rosemarie Hilde shook her head.

Ilse smiled happily.

'And Grannie?'

'No.'

'They are the nicest children in the world, Maurice,' said Rosemarie Ilse.

Just then the maid came in with the dishes.

Rosemarie Ilse still could not understand why Maurice had to drag his subordinates home with him. Surely they were entitled to have a few moments to themselves, just the two of them.

Binde was staring unseeingly into a corner of the room where a vase with artificial flowers was standing. Better be careful about palling up with Herz, he said to himself. But that was only a side-stream of the turgid, muddy flow of thought whose limpid waves conjured up the image of the ugly old woman in the little shop on L Avenue.

He felt the eyes of his hostess resting upon him. His own glided along the white tablecloth, as though running away. Fat lump! he thought.

Rosemarie Ilse's mother then made her appearance, an old lady with a pince-nez on a silver chain, all dressed in black up to her neck, with small yellow pieces of lace on her sleeves.

'Good evening,' she said.

All of them replied to the greeting, Werner Binde even getting up from his chair, only Herz nodded silently.

It was evident that the old lady did not feel a great deal of affection for the master of the house. Indeed, she considered Herz a rather rough man. Once she had seen her daughter removing a red stain from the sleeve of his uniform. Since then she was the prey of disturbing notions, but she never plucked up enough courage to ask Ilse what it was.

As for Herz, if it occurred to him that he did not like the old woman, he put the cause down to the relationship. Even a decent woman could be a bad mother-in-law. Her son, Rosemarie Ilse's brother, was at the front as a fairly highly-placed Nazi official. He could have been safely somewhere in the rear, but had volunteered to stay in the front line. The old woman was not too proud of it, and her remarks sometimes almost drove him to fury.

The old lady sat down in a spacious armchair in the middle and put a sewing-basket in her lap.

The maid started to serve dinner.

The conversation was sporadic and uneasy, Binde's presence being the obvious cause. Herz admitted it to himself and was vexed. The similarity between the name of the uncle and the driver was all poppycock, he said to himself, and he saw that Rosemarie Ilse's mother was just as annoyed as her daughter. Then Rosemarie Ilse complained that the cinema, where there had been a breakdown yesterday, was still not in order. The talk touched on new films and Rosemarie Ilse commented:

'My God, there's nothing but the war in all of them.'

Her mother nodded agreement, now and again looking Werner Binde over from under her pince-nez.

'It's getting quite unbearable at times,' added Rosemarie Ilse.

Herz fixed his eyes on her, severe and reproachful. He was watching carefully how Binde was reacting to it all. But the driver was fully occupied in the troublesome business of picking the bone of his leg of chicken.

'Germany is an empire that can wage and survive a ten times bigger war than this one, if need be,' said Herz.

Little Adolf agreed eagerly.

E

'All the same,' Rosemarie Ilse went on dreamily, her mouth full of food, 'I'd much rather have singing and dancing in my films. Oh, how gay we used to be, Maurice! We had such lovely times.'

Herz felt his face suffuse with blood. He'd like to slap the silly cow – why must she talk such drivel.

'Those times are gone,' said Binde. 'And heaven knows what's in store for us.'

'That's right, Binde,' said Herz; but he was not sure what exactly the driver meant.

'But surely you're not going to be in the war for ever,' protested Rosemarie Ilse. 'After all, you must get something out of it for yourselves.'

'I had a letter from the Hochfellers in Düsseldorf today,' said the old lady. 'Their house has been wrecked by an English bomb.'

'That is the lot of Germany at war,' said Herz, replying as it were to his wife's earlier statement (if the cow would only keep her trap shut) and glaring sternly at his mother-in-law.

The old lady rose, offended.

'I am going to bed,' she said.

After a while Werner Binde got up, too. He did not feel altogether at his ease with the Herzs. He left his fruit salad untouched, thanked them for the dinner, and said good-night. He left full of doubt whether the evening had been good for anything, and even supposing it had, whether things were not bad just the same.

He started the car, switched on the muffled blue lights and, with an uncertain feeling inside him, drove the car along the yellow fence that bordered the ghetto at the place where the road cut through it, to the garage of the H.Q.

3

Some ten minutes later that same evening Herz walked into his study in the upper left wing of the villa. He sat down behind a large mahogany table and carefully got ready his writing utensils. With slow, deliberate movements he took a sheet of glazed paper, a bottle of light blue ink, and a wooden penholder ornamented with burnt stripes. After a short deliberation, having, as he told himself, thought it all out in advance, he wrote a letter to the Third Department of the Berlin Gestapo.

He set his suspicions down in detail, underlining what were sentiments inspired by his fond regard for the welfare of the Third Reich rather than tangible proofs. He put one word down after another with painstaking care, as though they were not words but stones in a building he was erecting. The ideas behind the words took up all his thoughts. It was no longer a letter he was writing, it was a fort he was building, and it was necessary to eliminate all loopholes which might not remain unnoticed, and to strengthen the embrasures in case a hidden enemy should try to squeeze his impudent elbows into them. Finally he expressed quite openly his suspicion that the present commandant of the Terezín ghetto was, before the decisive year 1933, a member of a leftish trade union organization, just as most of the other members of the staff of the Europa café in Cologne, in which Heinz Albert Ritsche had worked as a waiter. It was a daring, indeed a highly dangerous, attack – Herz was fully aware of that. In fact, an unpleasant comparison came to him as he thought about it: if someone were to make such an attack against him, Herz would not know how to defend himself. Words of denunciation were at a great advantage these days: they were invariably the first. He suppressed a chill which had begun to tingle his spine and, with the aid of a wave of anger which he always found it easy to invoke, persuaded himself that all was fair in war. After all, it wasn't decent of Berlin to send in a new man when the old commandant, Wolf Seidl, left, was it? And if the erstwhile commandant was now at the front which offered him the possibility of a hero's death, was that not chiefly due to his, Herz's, letters and reports? Yes, almost everything spoke for him. Perhaps it would not then be altogether ill-considered if the High Command were to appoint him, Maurice Herz, commandant of the ghetto. He raised his pen for the final full stop as though it were a spear with which he wished to stab Heinz Albert Ritsche. Then he signed himself with a flourish. He folded the letter and put it in the envelope, heated the sealing-wax, and carved his initials, M.H., into the small mound.

He waited a few moments, then pushed the letter underneath a bronze paper-weight. It was a statuette of Atlas carrying the globe on his shoulders. To Maurice Herz it was a material symbol of his dream. He stroked the lifeless bronze with his eyes. Why should he now believe it completely out of the question that he would gain his ends? He had once already come so close . . . I have helped to build this hole, he thought as he gazed out excitedly at the darkened ghetto, this God-forsaken Jewish lair, ever since 'forty-one. At that time they had meted out punishment not only with their fists, but with hempen cord. In his mind's eye he saw the number seventeen. That's how many there were of them, and he had shot the only one to break loose, without the commandant's orders. It had been a good joke to appoint a Jewish hangman for the executions. No, he mustn't allow himself to be pushed around! The time had come to say: Enough! He started pacing up and down the room. Bringing Binde, he thought, had not been such a good idea. As for that silly goose, Rosemarie Ilse, she deserved a kick in the pants. Her twaddle was lately driving him crazy, just as the idiotic chatter of her mother, the aristocratic bitch. Between the two of them they'd get him into a concentration camp one of these days, he thought darkly.

The sealing-wax was reflected on the bronze surface of the statuette. It had set some time ago, and the initials M.H. looked like sharp incisions. But still Maurice Herz did not come down to his bedroom on the ground floor. He was gazing at the statuette and at the white envelope, thinking out a plan of campaign whose tentacles penetrated every nook and cranny in the white building of the H.Q., enveloping everything and everybody. He saw himself in a variety of places, behind the commandant's desk and in his villa, at the head of his colleagues sitting round the carved table at the Casino, as well as in Berlin, in new silver epaulettes, making his report which would serve as a model of military brevity and precision: destroyed. Destroyed and annihilated.

It was late in the night before he went to bed.

4

The people who passed by the little shop on L Avenue that evening, trying to look as though the afternoon that had just passed was a normal part of the ghetto's routine, were nevertheless in a hurry. It was clearly to be seen that no one had the least inclination to wander about in the ghetto. And since they had prudently vanished from the streets at the time of Maurice Herz's and Werner Binde's visit, many of them must have wondered why, on this particular summer evening, the shop 'The Sun' was still open. However, none of those to whom this occurred ventured inside, while Joachim Spiegel, the only one who would certainly have called, did not dare even to set foot in Rose Street. The sentry who came on later did not notice, and people had other things to think about than how to enlarge their wardrobe by the addition of torn stockings or stoles. The Jewish sentries paced their beats slowly and with pretended assurance for only short distances from their posts, so that no one came to know about Elizabeth Feiner, who was still lying inside the shop. Thus no report of the incident was included in the Jewish elder's report and was therefore not among the documents which were next day presented to commandant Heinz Albert Ritsche. And Herz's efforts came to nothing.

It was a little before this, at about the time Maurice Herz finally went to sleep, that Elizabeth Feiner came to. It would be an exaggeration to say that after those six hours she completely regained consciousness; everything seemed to give way beneath her and to swim in darkness. An unpleasant whistling noise sounded in her ears, mingling with the shouts of children, which called her 'Auntie', and changing to the piercing shriek of a locomotive's whistle, then to the wailing of dozens of sirens and, at the same time, to steam-rollers which kept running over her forehead with their rough-surfaced, heavy wheels. Suddenly she found it revolting to lie helplessly on the floor boards. When she at last picked herself up and laboriously got to her feet, she did not know for a long time what time it was. All round her there was nothing but silence. It must be time for her to pull down the shutters. It was also dark, which meant that it was after the curfew and thus impossible for any Jew to appear in the streets. Her dazed mind conjured up images of a long-forgotten, distant childhood, of nights when she had been afraid to go out in the dark and frightened when she awoke up in her bed in the middle of the night. Now, too, she was afraid, but for different reasons. She wished that the darkness should swallow everything and that the rough, opaque curtain which seemed to hang in front of her eyes should never be raised. And she wished that Joachim Spiegel might be somewhere near at that last moment which would put an end to all the troubles of this world. She immediately rebuked herself, however; she must not link anyone with her misfortune. She realized that she could not stand long on her feet without support, so she sat down on the floor. She longed to be able to close her eyes and sleep off everything that had happened if she was to survive it and to go on living. Thus she sat, her former ideas, according to which a human being could keep his dignity even in this place, shattered and ruined like a wretched pile of debris. Worst of all, an evil thought fought its way through to the surface of her consciousness, searing her brain; had the red-faced officer who had knocked her down not even for a moment seen in her his own mother? The reply which seemed to roar inside her transformed her face so that it now resembled that of an ugly, astonished child. She knew only one thing for certain: that she must not leave the shop in the night. She therefore remained sitting where she was, feeling her legs, her face, and her whole body with her hands. Each touch she felt in the marrow of her bones. But this time, painful though it was, she no longer succeeded in fainting. She had to squat on the cold planks of the floor, alone with the mice and her own, now wide-awake consciousness.

The night passed slowly and heavily. It was like a chilly blanket of darkness retaliating for the hot day. Not even the faint rays of the yet distant dawn, nor the bluish glow of the stars which she could see through the windows of the shop, could penetrate this blanket.

5

The morning was foggy. From inside the shop the figures flitting past on the other side of the greasy paper in the window like a grotesque shadow play of L Avenue appear only as a monotonous pantomime of heads. It is difficult to make out just how much they are bent under their broad-brimmed hats. The shiny metal or bamboo sticks of umbrellas herald a wet autumn, the rain and the damp mists, which come early in this region, bringing confirmation. The paper is soon soaked through with rain, and before she pulls down the corrugated iron shutters Elizabeth Feiner takes down the paper and leaves it to dry overnight on the counter.

Her angular head, even more scarred with bluish veins, large and small, than it was before the end of the summer, looked as though the blood inside it was getting darker. She was racking her brains with a single question, precise and yet ramified at the same time. A few blows were enough to put out that which burns in human beings from beginning to end, to become the beacon which we call conscience.

She was now in the habit of sitting motionless on a low stool, as though the contradiction between the depths of her experience and the heights of her resolutions, which had swallowed up everything, had consumed her as well. Thus she would forget that she was not alone.

With her in the shop was Ruth, Joachim Spiegel's niece, who had arrived with the August transport, a month after the SS visit in July, while her parents had remained in Kassel, one of them being an Aryan. She had not heard from them for two whole months. How was Elizabeth Feiner to explain to her why her parents had stayed at home in Kassel while she was here? Would Ruth be able to understand that, according to the Nuremberg laws, there were two kinds of human blood?

She treated Ruth with a curious kind of consideration which took the form of silence. Now she was staring at the small, thin girl, whose soft, dark hair sprouted up from a sallow forehead and whose white teeth were rather spaced out and almost transparent, as though they were made of ivory. The girl's face with its inquisitive black eyes, such as she once used to have herself, seemed to her to represent a future reproach, for something that not even Elizabeth Feiner was able to give a name to was marking the child's face with the sorrowful expression that Jewish children so frequently have. This reproach at her own constant silence was mixed up with a feeling of gratitude, Ruth being the only one to come these days, as the ghetto was in the throes of an influenza epidemic and many children were ill.

Ruth played with the stoles, straightening them out with her thin, long fingers. After a while she became tired of the silence.

'Auntie Feiner,' she said, 'why don't you keep the fire going?'

The dark silence which had depressed her but which she herself was unable to break was shattered at last.

'There's nothing to keep it going with,' she replied. 'I've burned everything.'

She couldn't touch the few pieces of furniture that had been left in the place. Where would she put the things if she did? And what if the owner of the barber's shop were to return one day?

The little girl was not satisfied, however. She pouted, this childish grimace contrasting strangely with her grave, grown-up eyes; the white expanse of teeth, the two front ones at the top thrusting forward a little, was parted restlessly. She and Auntie Feiner were in the habit of composing verses.

> 'The sun has flown far from our street;
>   Now snow is there;
> Like slippers white beneath our feet,
>   For us to wear.'

But they knew this one by heart now. Perhaps they could try to compose some new lines.

It rained all the time, thought Elizabeth Feiner in an effort to distract her thoughts in another direction. Winter was coming. But what were they going to do if the winter came so soon? And why was she not saying all this out loud?

'I'll tell you a story,' she said at last.

Ruth nodded.

'Once upon a time there was an evil man,' she began. 'He wanted to rule the whole wide world. Nobody loved him, and he was angry about it and so he sent his subjects to the hangman to be executed, one by one . . .'

She did not realize that she had stopped speaking and there was silence again.

'But Auntie Feiner,' protested Ruth. 'It's not finished yet.'

'Yes, that's just the trouble, child,' said Elizabeh Feiner.

Then she burst out, so suddenly and so urgently that Ruth was startled and opened her mouth with the small mouse-like teeth:

'I'll tell you the rest tomorrow. You must leave me alone now. Go on, run home, Ruth!'

Her voice was so gritty and unkind and there was so much urgency in it that it frightened her.

'I know who the evil man is, anyway . . .' said Ruth.

'Go on, run . . .'

Elizabeth Feiner shook all over until the door closed behind the girl. Her mind was filled with a single question. What would happen when the door opened again to admit a greenish-grey uniform with the reddish face. It was not finished yet. That was what troubled her so much. Whatever happened, she had to be alone, she told herself.

On several occasions during the time when the pale glow of the sun was obliterated by rain, from the beginning to the end of October, she had thought of going to the Council of Elders to hand over the keys of the shop to someone else. She did not wish to remain here any longer. But she hardly ever got farther than halfway up the stairs. She would like to scrub the pavements as she used to do. There was nothing to be ashamed of in that. It was only when she saw that reddish face with its tight-lipped mouth in front of her that she knew whence humiliation came. Would she succeed in getting away from here before they arrived? She had sixty-two years of life behind her, she did not make hasty decisions. And yet she had changed her mind every time just before she got there. There was something else to be taken into account; someone would have to take her place. Perhaps Joachim Feiner – oh, she admonished herself, how silly of her, that wasn't his name! Both these things were rooted deeply within her, the idiotic desire for human company and sympathy, and the repudiation of this desire. She mustn't tie anyone to herself, and yet, it was so sad to be alone. So she wavered between her resolve to hand over the keys and her repeated last-minute withdrawals. She toyed with the idea, recurrent like the ebb and tide, that if the expected commission from a neutral country arrived before the two SS men, it would be composed entirely of young people, in whom she would be able to confide. She thought back to that summer morning, the rosy day, and the night in which she was unable to get up from the floor. She was glad she had sent Ruth away. It was windy outside, and a slight drizzle wafted from the mountains was washing away the last traces of summer's beauty. It looked as if it was going to start raining in earnest.

She felt tired. Intending to sit down on her white stool,

she stopped dead halfway, her shoulders hunched in a stooping posture. Someone was standing outside the shop. Now he was about to enter. And although it flashed across her mind for a mere fraction of a second that it might be Joachim Spiegel, she was not surprised to see the green cloth, flecked with countless grey spots. She was not frightened even when Werner Binde carefully closed the door behind him, leaving his hand to rest on the handle for a while. She was only conscious of an uncertain feeling of expectancy.

Werner Binde shook off the rain. He felt none too brave. He was on his way back from the building in which was the Council of Elders and had stopped here, in front of the little shop on L Avenue. 'The Sun' – a stone sun with its rays sharply chiselled above the door, that was a barrier beyond which he was reluctant to penetrate. The passers-by saw this, because he had hesitated a little they immediately vacated his side of the street. He failed to observe this, however, because as soon as he entered the shop and as soon as he left it again and hurried on through the town, he was sure that no one except Elizabeth Feiner had noticed him, since the pavements on both sides were again crowded.

'Good day,' he said.

She regarded him distrustfully. Was the greeting only a polite ruse? She took off her spectacles, then said: 'Good day.'

She could not bring herself to ask boldly what it was the soldier wanted, despite the fact that something was impelling her to ask just that question. She was puzzled by his calmness and by the look in his cold, quiet eyes.

Werner Binde was standing face to face with the old woman's angular head, bewhiskered chin, and red root of the nose.

And Elizabeth Feiner, waiting all the time for what was to come, could not make out what was concealed behind the soldier's fish-like eyes. She had no idea that the very fact that he was here had a certain meaning, that it meant the result of a three months' invisible struggle against Maurice Herz.

Werner Binde has come to see the old woman whom Herz
had humiliated. This was a climax, the transformation of a
wish into action. He did not like Herz, thinking it was because
here Herz punctuated every sentence with a slap, while at H.Q.
he acted the perfect gentleman. That, Werner Binde said to
himself, is just what I can't stand. He had resented it, already
in the case of Erich von Stumpke and Oswald Trautenfelder,
with whom he used to drive out to inspect the stores supplied
by the Mauthausen camp and used for the purposes of the
Winterhilfe for South Germany. He was hardly aware that this
feeling of distaste dated back to the time when he met his own
step-brother, Fritz, in Buchenwald. He was not allowed as
much as to shake his hand or throw him a handerchief with
which to bandage his wounds. Fritz died in front of his eyes
like some beast, and he, Werner, had smiled inanely so that
no one should see that he was in any way concerned about
the bloody bundle of flesh which had been suspected of a non-
sensical offence – that of listening to foreign radio stations.

Elizabeth Feiner debated with herself: should I ask, or
not?

Werner Binde searched his mind to find out whether there
was something that drew him to this ugly, old woman with
the prominent cheek-bones and with grey hairs on her chin
and under her nose. He did not dare to dwell on the idea of
what the others would think of him standing here inactive
like this.

Elizabeth Feiner was suddenly disturbed by a feeling that
the silence was about to blow up like a load of dynamite.
When was it going to start?

But Werner Binde was thinking of other things. He did not
wish to play with the word *coward,* and yet it was this very
word that haunted him ever since that July evening when he
had dinner with Maurice Herz and his wife. It had all started
with that silly dinner. Nevertheless, Werner Binde knew very
well that there was something that had happened before the
dinner. And everything after it. On the following day the soldiers had received a tin of sardines each, brought from Portu-

gal via Switzerland. He could not eat his sardines, even though at the time he had only a vague idea of what he was going to do with them and did not want to admit it even to himself. So he carried them around in his pocket, knowing very well that he intended to give them to this old woman. He had only been looking for a suitable opportunity. 'I feel nothing towards her,' he kept repeating to himself, 'absolutely nothing, she is only old and ugly.' Yet, he had never carried out his intention. There was a barrier in his way, an obstacle that was fully and precisely described by the word *cowardice*. It was not only that he was afraid of prying eyes – they could be put off the scent in a number of ways, all of them foolproof. He could, for instance, pretend to beat the old woman and then leave the sardines here as if by accident; he could be at hand in the vicinity of the shop when she went to open up in the morning. But he rejected them all. They did not afford him that which he was seeking: satisfaction once and for all. That satisfaction however, did not come even now that he was at last standing here almost feeling her breath upon him. The old woman, he saw clearly, was afraid of him. She could not look inside his soul. There was no reason why he should feel anything for her, she was merely a mediator between him and his future peace of mind. All the same, he could not rid himself of the worrying thought that this which he had dared to do would never be properly appreciated. He stood there in front of her, quiet and subdued, disappointment staring out of his eyes; he looked into hers, sunken and old, and read in them a combination of fear and defiance and a profound resignation. She was not as ugly as he had imagined her all this time. And yet – she was ripe for the crematorium. One blow would do the trick. He was furious with himself for thinking like this. He turned quickly to look at the entrance. Nobody there. He looked at his watch, hardly knowing why he did so. He was jumpy, he told himself. Out of the pocket of his greatcoat he pulled the tin and, thinking suddenly that all this fuss was useless, that he should have been rougher, should have simply handed the thing over and nothing more, he left as unexpectedly as he had come, almost without a greeting, perhaps a little nervously, walking out of the shop with his rolling, sailor's gait.

Elizabeth Feiner was left looking at the spot where he had been standing, at the greasy paper that replaced the glass. She stood thus for a long time, uncomprehending. The dynamite did not go off, then. She had, nevertheless, not failed to register the moment when the soldier had been on the point of hitting her. She could not pluck up courage to touch the sardines in their gaudy yellow wrapping. What if the soldier's shadow appeared again on the paper in the window? And yet, something told her that he would not come back. Had it perhaps been fear that had made him glance at his watch and at the door? But fear was attentiveness intensified and only rarely was it transmuted into action, fear was merely the transformation of one's own thoughts into those of the enemy. She pushed the tin away in loathing, under the stoles hanging down in folds from the ceiling. She was confused. As so often before, it again occurred to her that one had always something to learn, that no final impression was ever accurate, because as long as events were being uncoiled from the spool of life no impression was really final. Who could tell what people were like underneath their shell of coarseness or despair where only they themselves could see, sometimes not even they. Where then lay the boundaries that divided people? Unthinkingly she reached out for the sardines.

She went out of the shop and pulled down the shutters. Then she opened the old, black silk, man's umbrella whose great width was quite out of proportion to her emaciated figure, clad in a dark blue dress with grey, opaque buttons. In her shiny fish-scale handbag with its brass clasps she carried the yellow tin of sardines in oil, that strange gift which she could not as yet comprehend.

Halfway up Rose Street she changed her direction. She felt feverish, as if a flame was burning her up from within and she was unable to fight against it. Wasn't the whole thing merely a trap? Was it permissible for a woman who was trained as

she was, and as were all the other people herded together in
the ghetto, to accept something that rightfully belonged to
pure-blooded soldiers? But yet another voice inside her was
asking why Binde had been so careful and quiet. And the first
voice answered: that's just a mask! The sardines had become
a source of disquiet, a time bomb planted on her soul.

She saw it all again, as it had been three months ago and
as it had been today. Two men were in the shop, one red-
faced and indifferent, his head a little flattened, like a beet-
root. The other one had only acted roughly in one instance, by
telling her to shut up. But perhaps even that was intended to
help her. It was all so very complicated. Why, after today's
encounter, did she want to think well of him, as though it
were out of the question that there should be a trick in it
somewhere? The red-faced one had beaten her, and he would
have done so even if she had kept quiet. The old proverb
about the dog and the stick came to her mind.

No, she would not go straight to the barracks.

She made for a square building with two crossed horses'
heads in a coat of arms above a stone doorway – the house of
the Council of Elders.

The street, it seemed to her, was not level, it wound itself
round the trees, up and down like a great swing, and the people were laughing at the sight. She touched her head; it was
burning. She could not stand it if Binde were to come to her
today, or even tomorrow, she thought. After all, it was not
only the blows and the kicks – there was something else be-
sides that. She was at the mercy of her own thoughts, which
her brain shot at her heart and she was helpless to prevent it.
She would tell the Council of Elders that her involuntary service was at an end. She would hand over the keys. Good-bye
to 'The Sun'! Yes, that would rid her of the worry of what
would happen if she were unable to go to the shop tomorrow.

She trotted through the town, perseveringly, under her huge
umbrella, the rents in which permitted the wind to blow the
rain in and to soak her more than could be healthy for an old,
sick woman.

At last she reached the house with the coat of arms.

The staircase with its high steps resembled a pyramid. With difficulty she raised one foot and then the other, one foot and the other, and again and again, so that she lost all count of time as she struggled up and up until she stopped in front of the Chief Administrator's desk. She did not even know how she signed the written declaration saying that the shop, 'The Sun', was in perfect order, nor was she aware of the searching gaze of the man to whom she handed the keys. All she knew was that he was kind and that he agreed with her in everything.

'Just a moment, Mrs Feiner,' he was saying, his voice sounding as if it came from a long way off. 'I'll see you to the door.'

'Yes . . .'

'Just a moment, I shan't be a minute.'

But Elizabeth Feiner did not hear him. She was already walking down the stairs.

The barracks in which she lived were not far – just across the road, standing there along steep slopes that towered up in the twilight and fell on the other side into the depths of a different world which was no longer the ghetto.

She could not remember when she had last felt so ill. Every intake of breath hurt her. Pleurisy, she thought. But it could also be just 'flu. Notwithstanding the pain, she managed an inward smile. Just. What a silly word!

She was already halfway home before the rain-soaked administrator caught up with her

'Really, Mrs Feiner!' he was saying. 'Why didn't you wait for me?'

She looked at him, puzzled. She couldn't for the life of her think of his name.

She went on taking short steps and not noticing that the man was supporting her.

At the door the Chief Administrator had to leave her.

'Good night . . .'

She thought she nodded her head in farewell. Or at least she wanted to.

She placed the small, shiny tin underneath her pillow, took off her shoes, and lay down. She closed her eyes straightaway, and then pulled the blanket over her head. She wouldn't tell anyone – the other women might be afraid of infection. An indescribable weight was constantly upon her. The end was approaching. That delusive game which she had called life would soon be over. And just on such a remarkable day. The stone portal of the window, with its thin, rusty bars set close to one another, was jumping up and down before her closed eyes. On the other side of the room was a real, red-hot stove, surrounded by a swarm of women preparing supper. 'Room 38', peopled by the evening, full of children and visitors. And from outside she could hear the water swirling in the drain-pipe, and thought of Joachim Spiegel's niece, who recited:

> ' The sun has flown far from our street;
> Now snow is there . . .'

The arrows kept on coming. Now they came from afar and embedded themselves in the centre of her forehead. The autumn and its rains should not have set in. Not yet. She fell asleep, willing herself to sleep so eagerly that an unpleasant, sticky perspiration sprang up all over her body. She was completely covered by the blanket, out of whose torn, ragged end small grey feathers kept fluttering and were then carried upwards by the draught, towards the ceiling.

6

That evening Maurice Herz was already at home. Rosemarie Ilse was somewhat excited, and the way she ran about the kitchen made Herz think of everything that he had so successfully brought into play. Events had taken an unexpected turn. Rosemarie Ilse looked at him frequently, her eyes – in contrast to the confused haste with which she hopped

F

round the table – full of gratitude, brilliant and devoted. Maurice had been named Heinz Albert Ritsche's adjutant, to the dismay of all the wives of the other SS officers, who were jealous of her. As far as he was concerned, he was quite content with this new appointment, considering it to be the embryo of his future promotions. True, the Party's special plenipotentiary, who had recently paid a visit to the ghetto to supervise the preparations for the visit from Switzerland, had, in the course of a private talk, made it clear to Herz that the thing with the trade unions and the commandant was unfounded; at the same time, however, he had told Herz that the Third Department commended him on his vigilance. 'You are a man who uses his eyes and ears,' he said. 'That's the kind of man we like.' I've undoubtedly strengthened my position, thought Herz. A special plenipotentiary would not have come to tell him if it had been otherwise. It, of course, immediately occurred to him that the fellow in black had not spilled everything he knew. But he at once rejected this idea, which undermined the pillars upon which his satisfaction rested, imparting to him the notion that the plenipotentiary might likewise have told Ritsche everything. They trusted him! That was clear! Well, he would not disappoint them. At the party that was held in the evening the plenipotentiary had honoured him with special attention. He was tall and slim, in a black uniform, his personality devoid of the menace which was no doubt inherent in his mission. Herz felt on top of the world. Had it not been for this, he would never have done what he had done just now. His decision was truly born of a momentary impulse: he had, at an opportune moment, invited both the commandant and the plenipotentiary 'for a little dinner' to his villa. The plenipotentiary had excused himself with a smile. It looked as if he really regretted his inability to accept the invitation; but he was leaving that very night. Ritsche, however, had accepted. And thus, for the second time in less than a quarter of a year, Maurice Herz had infringed the unwritten rules of the Nazi hierarchy: the first time from the bottom, by inviting Binde, and now from the top – that was more daring and, it struck him, more dangerous. When he had done it, he had of course had quite a lot of French cognac inside him. But in any case, he told himself as he thought the whole thing over, if you risk nothing you gain nothing.

The lion's share of this evening's success fell to Rosemarie Ilse, who, even though she was not in the least initiated into the threads that had set in motion the impetuous gesture of invitation, was fully aware of the greatness of the moment. She did not know what to do first. The chickens had not yet arrived from the refrigerator, and she had no time left to distribute the flowers in the vases. She wouldn't make do with artificial ones today, of course! Since the day when she had to let the maid-servant, Greta, go because the silly wench had applied to serve on the eastern front, she was continually on the go. No time to do anything. And even if Maurice did not say much, she could see what high hopes he had of tonight's dinner. He sat by the stove, warming his feet, his reddish, powdered face showing how intensively he was thinking.

Every now and again Maurice Herz would rub his temples with the palms of his hands. He could not make himself out. Were there in him two personalities, one of them daring and enterprising, yes, you might even say rapacious, in its desire to climb to the top, and the other timid and self-effacing, constantly realizing the fact that he was nothing but an unfinished house-painter's apprentice? Both these Herzs were now waiting for the big occasion. To the first it seemed that the drops of water which drizzled persistently from the skies were turning the wheels on his behalf. The second doubted that the commandant would come at all. Perhaps he had not wanted to say anything in front of the plenipotentiary, but now he would show him who was whose superior and who was only an unfinished house-painter. After all, said Herz to himself, an adjutant was only an adjutant. An adjutant must not jump too high or he might slip and fall. But, he rebuked himself, the game was on. Now it was necessary to rake in the trumps.

He gazed into the fire. His disquiet quickly vanished. The plenipotentiary's favour was a card well worth having. And, seeing that Rosemarie Ilse kept hopping around the stove like a goat, he said, languidly: 'Plenty of time.'

When at last the car's brakes were heard in front of the villa, everything was in its place.

Heinz Albert Ritsche was a small, stoutish man wearing gold-rimmed spectacles on a white, fleshy nose. Altogether he resembled a business man rather than a high SS officer. As a matter of fact nobody knew how he had managed to gain his position in the rear. The subject was never mentioned, however, as any undue curiosity would most probably have resulted in the questioners being sent to the front themselves, and that was a possibility that appealed to no one. It was just this, though, that gave Ritsche a flattering aura of mystery which for others, including Herz, represented an easy target.

They ate in silence. Herz was at a loss to discover the cause of this taciturnity. The dinner over, Ritsche laid aside his napkin and said he had enjoyed the meal.

'Did you really?' asked Rosemarie Ilse, pleased, but slightly disconcerted by the reserved manner of their distinguished guest.

'Yes, really, thank you,' said Ritsche.

The children came into the drawing-room.

'Uncle Ritsche,' shouted little Adolf, 'I want to scalp ten Jewish pigs!'

'You're not old enough yet,' Herz told him, smiling.

He turned to the commandant, still a little uneasy: 'Children, Herr Kommandant, they're the hope of Germany.'

Ritsche nodded his satisfaction. It sounded good; the hope of Germany.

Now it seemed to Herz that the barrier of ice had been breached. He would be damned if he would do it a second time, though. In the next instant, however, he felt a warm glow of satisfaction at having invited the commandant.

Little Hilda asked: 'Have Jews got children too?'

Rosemarie Ilse smiled happily: 'Oh, Lord, how clever these children are!'

Herz's satisfaction increased every minute. I was right, after all, he thought. This was the kind of easy-going comradeship he had in mind all along, the kind that as a rule was not without its effect on service relations. He was convinced that this impression was correct. What he needed was to gain Ritsche's confidence, then he would be able to make his weight felt far more than hitherto. He would have an invisible pillar against which to lean. It occurred to him at the same time that in these days, so troublesome for the Reich, personal wrangles were highly undesirable. He would not be disappointed even if the only outcome of his plan was to be a closer friendship between the two of them. It struck him suddenly, and pleasurably, that now, as adjutant, he was actually able to view things from a loftier standpoint, on a higher scale.

Rosemarie Ilse, her cheeks full of colour, wore a black silk dress and a white apron which she kept taking off and putting on again. She was under the impression that she looked particularly good in that apron, and in the end she left it on. To Ritsche, her neck-less body seemed comical. The neck got lost somewhere when she was being born, he thought. After the plenipotentiary had left, he had debated with himself for a long time whether to accept the invitation or not. He had not liked the way those two talked together, and could not rid himself of the idea that the red-faced nosy parker had been assigned to spy on him. In the end he had come, but he had not capitulated; he was merely reconnoitring in enemy territory. In order to keep a certain, not too offensive, distance, he had left his wife at home. The devoted glances bestowed on him by Herz's wife he found unpleasant. What an impossible cow, he said to himself. What does she think she is doing, staring at me like that?

Rosemarie Ilse felt that the commandant was looking her over. She leant towards him across the table and, taking courage, blurted out with a girlish giggle:

'You are men, but in your uniforms you look like boys.'

The bitch, thought Ritsche.

After a while he said, aloud: 'We can well be proud of our women. They're our second reserve.'

That was the only thing that occurred to him.

Rosemarie Ilse thought: Mother was right to stay upstairs – every conversation in this house is bound to end with the reserve, the front, and the war. When they had told her who was coming, she had excused herself and had her dinner taken up to her room.

'But, Herr Kommandant,' said Rosemarie Ilse, 'you'll never let them get as far as this, will you?'

He realized at once what she was driving at.

'Our Führer,' he said, irritated, 'has several times spoken on the subject, and he has left no room for doubt. It is completely out of the question. If you ask your husband, he is sure to set your mind at rest on that score.'

Herz threw a worried look in Ritsche's direction .

The joyful, intoxicated feeling, which had taken hold of Rosemarie Ilse and had made her happy all through the dinner, was gone.

Herz realized that the commandant might think that he was neglecting his wife, or even might wonder why she was still not working as other officer's wives.

'We have already talked about it, haven't we, Ilse?' he said quickly.

She fixed desperate eyes on her husband. What had they already talked about? Oh, God, let her not spoil anything. She couldn't remember. And even she knew very well that these political discussions were no joking matter.

Maurice Herz's reddish face changed its colour to blue. The bloody bitch! But he kept his temper and, mistakenly interpreting the commandant's silence as agreement, he said: 'Ilse and I have often thought that perhaps she might work on the requisitioning commission . . .'

If the idiot has invited me because of this, thought Ritsche, then he might have saved himself the trouble. Let him send his fat sow where he likes.

Rosemarie Ilse was offended. How silly to lie like that. Surely they didn't have to resort to lies. Was she supposed to go to the Jewesses, like that ginger-haired Herta? Did perhaps Maurice think she didn't have enough on her hands as it was? Why were they fighting the war, in that case? She almost started to cry on the spot.

'That is very commendable,' said Ritsche. 'Your children are growing fast, and anyway, you can always take a Czech maid.'

'Never!' cried Rosemarie Ilse. 'They're so terribly lazy. And apart from that, I couldn't stand a Jewess in my flat. I simply couldn't.'

'I'd throw her out, Mummie,' put in little Adolf. 'You'd let me throw her out, wouldn't you?'

Heinz Albert Ritsche got up suddenly. 'It is very pleasant here,' he said, 'but I must go now.'

Herz did not fail to notice how cold, curt, and stiff were his words.

They saw him to the car.

It was Herz's Mercedes-Benz, which he had sent that afternoon to fetch Ritsche. Werner Binde stood by the car's door, and he saluted them with his fish-like eyes.

'It was a great honour, Herr Kommandant,' said Herz.

Suddenly he felt terribly small, stupid and vile. No, he should not have played about with that invitation.

Ritsche, on the other hand, lounging comfortably in his seat, did not seem to be thinking along such serious lines as Herz.

Back in the house, Rosemarie Ilse told herself that no one invited Maurice with such a show of politeness. With belated tears in her eyes she flared up at him:

'It's not enough for you that the maid has gone, that I slave away like a nigger from morning till night, is it? What a fool I was to marry you . . .'

'Don't be daft!' Herz replied in irritation. 'The requisitioning commission is child's play. And you'll pick up all sorts of useful things for yourself.'

He was furious with her, and if it weren't for the children, he would have slapped her. But it was just as well, at least let him have peace and quiet at home. No, Maurice Herz did not have sufficient self-assurance tonight. The meek one inside him was on top. Wasn't it better to be small? He had to think things out.

Rosemarie Ilse came to the conclusion that there was some truth in what Maurice said. She'd take a dog with her to the ghetto. What was she to do with such an impossible husband, in such times, and . . . But she could think of nothing more. She stopped crying, powdered her face, and then went upstairs to talk to her mother and to confide her troubles. After a time she returned downstairs and went to bed.

7

A week later Werner Binde drove the members of the requisitioning commission – generally known under the nickname of 'grab-alls' – to the ghetto. Among them was Rosemarie Ilse Herz. He stopped to let them get out at various places according to a plan that had been drawn up beforehand. In the end he was left with the ginger-haired Herta, the gardener's wife, and with Rosemarie Ilse, who recalled that the driver had dined with them last summer, and asked him to be so kind and accompany her everywhere she went. Herta's Alsatian, Rex, sat huddled in a corner of the car, jumping up on to the window and barking all the time.

In accordance with the instructions he had received, Werner Binde stopped the car in front of the 'Hamburg' barracks, in which lived the women of Terezín.

He shambled behind Herta and Rosemarie Ilse along the corridors with the small balconies built in severe military style.

The two women were a long time deciding in which room to start their work, finally making up their minds to begin on the first floor, right in the corner. And so it happened that at about half-past nine in the morning they walked into Room 38, the room in which Elizabeth Feiner was lying.

The room was long and high, but the huge and cumbersome three-storey bunks filled it so completely that only a little space was left between the two rows.

Rosemarie Ilse did not feel too well in the stuffy, badly aired room. She kept darting quick glances to one side and another, and turning all the time, afraid that something or somebody might fly out at her. But as nothing happened, she grew used to it in a very short while. The only thing she saw on turning round were the eyes of Werner Binde; he was standing against the wall, almost motionless, staring ahead of himself with a vague expression on his face that might have signified indifference or even superciliousness.

She was ashamed, before herself as well as before the ginger-haired Herta, ashamed of being here and of being so clumsy. Where was she to start? And how was she to do it? Was she perhaps to rummage among those foul-smelling possessions, or in those filthy beds?

Just then she heard Herta give a slight scream.

'Is anybody here?'

Elizabeth Feiner's face took upon itself an almost imperceptible shade of astonishment, so slight that it was gone immediately; only her parchment-like skin, which had no further layer underneath, became slightly wrinkled around the eyes. For the seventh day running she was being burnt up by high fever. Something was devouring her from within, she was shrivelling up, she could resist no longer and was losing her strength.

In those seven days she had not once tried to solve the question that had worried her so much while she was still in the shop: whether she would withstand the onslaught on human dignity that the present time brought with it. The question only cropped up again now, though very feebly.

She lay staring at the yellowish ceiling, her hands under the blanket. It was not the ceiling she saw – it was a stretched-out cloth, with her life parading dimly across it, divided into years, weeks, and seconds. She saw a large school blackboard, on which invisible fingers drew the likeness of her father with his carefully tended ginger moustache, and a little girl rather like Joachim Spiegel's niece. All this was dim and yet somehow extremely clearly outlined. The little girl told her father a lie; instead of doing her homework she had been to visit a friend and then blamed her for her own omission. The father first wanted to strike her, but then he said: 'No, I shan't beat you, life will give you a worse spanking than I ever could. But don't lie again, ever. A human being should keep himself clean.' This picture is rapidly followed by a succession of others: scenes faintly remembered from childhood; the girl with the pigtails grows up and her skin terribly quickly becomes as yellow as the ceiling, her veins become blue and stand out on her forehead, reshaping her face into curious angles. Elizabeth Feiner recognises herself and opens her eyes.

At this moment Herta called out:

'Damn it all, is anyone here or not?'

Herta, of course, knew there was someone there. But she wanted to hear her own voice.

Elizabeth Feiner again saw in her mind's eye the shapeless and dull days in which she was in charge of the shop, 'The Sun'. Outside it was beautiful weather and inside it was dark. Then Rose Street and the former barber's shop was replaced by the moment when she relinquished the keys, that incarnation of a mission which had not led anywhere. Now the pictures grew hazy – all she saw was the ceiling, yellow, dark and depressing. Elizabeth Feiner at last discovered the answer to her question, the question of how to avoid humiliation: the answer was to remain silent.

The echo of Herta's words died away.

Elizabeth Feiner entered upon the threshold of a world which she had hitherto resisted. She no longer had the strength to keep death at bay by thoughts of the little girl; the only thing she knew was that from now on she was not going to speak any more. Reconciled with everything, she lay still, only her eyes roving round the room. From her bunk, low above the ground, she at once caught sight of the German women, the dog, and the soldier in the background. She could not make out his face because of the distance, and she was not altogether sure as to the size of the animal, either. But she had distinctly heard the penetrating voice of the German woman, and she had understood her words. Only now did she make any reply, quite quietly and only to herself, for she did not know how much strength she could spare to lend her voice; and in a way she wished that she alone and no one else might hear it. She narrowed her eyes to mere slits, trying to keep out vision and to prevent daylight from hurting them. The inspection did not concern her, she could still realize that much, for she had nothing at all that might be of interest to the living. She lay still, her head inclined to one side on a none too clean pillow, like someone who is losing a struggle that is being waged inside his body but is already out of reach of his spirit.

'You swine!' shrieked Herta. 'Are you dumb, or what? What're you doing, wallowing here in bed?'

Elizabeth Feiner did not reply. What was coming next? Why had she feared the fever in the long, cold nights when the wind howled outside? Thinking of the wind was pleasant, so cool and incredible. The rain was rattling on the rusty metal of the drain-pipe; she heard that now very distinctly. The rain!

'These lazy swine!' said Herta again. 'Nothing wrong with them, but they don't feel like work.'

Herta's voice was coarse and full of hatred. Elizabeth Feiner took no notice of it. Somewhere there were mountain slopes and somewhere there were roses. And elsewhere nothing.

Herta was a child of hatred. Her mother, herself alone in the world, had abandoned her, and later no one had come to take the little girl from the Berlin orphanage. Up to the age of eighteen she had been like a discarded thing that walked, breathed and spoke. Now at last she had found people who were lower than she, upon whom even she might trample. And thus she said what she did calmly and with a feeling of superiority, even though she saw that the woman in front of her had only a few steps to go to the end of her life.

'Frau Ilse,' she said. 'Go through her things and you'll see how these bitches can sham.'

Although she protested inwardly against this form of address, Rosemarie Ilse Herz nevertheless obediently, but with a feeling of revulsion she found it hard to overcome, bent down to the pieces of luggage under the sick woman's bunk, and opened them.

The top suitcase did not belong to Elizabeth Feiner, but to her neighbour. She was one of a numerous family, who kept all they had with their mother; a partly eaten stick of imitation Hungarian salami, two bagfuls of sugar, a cake of soap, and wedding rings in a box that used to hold a watch.

The dog barked, having smelt the meat, and Herta had to hold him back.

'There, you see!' she said.

Rosemarie Ilse threw the salami to the dog. He pounced on it eagerly, but found it too highly seasoned to devour all of it. Rosemarie Ilse was about to put back the things she had taken out of the suitcase, but Herta stopped her, saying:

'Oh, don't bother about that!'

Rosemarie Ilse was still not altogether at ease. She was unable to accustom herself so quickly to her new role, yet she had a feeling that if she were to come again (now she saw how silly she had been not to have come before) she would know what to do and how to do it. She had no doubt that when she was alone without curious eyes watching her, Herta picked up quite a few things that the Winterhilfe never saw! Those two gold wedding rings . . . Rosemarie Ilse was scared to think of it further.

'Frau Ilse,' Herta interrupted, 'you'd better look under the mattress, too.'

Rosemarie Ilse cautiously reached out towards the bunk and, as though she did not even wish to see the sick woman lying on it, gingerly picked up one corner of the pillow between her fingers; she tugged at it sharply, lifted it, and let it fall again.

There was a hollow, crunchy sound as Elizabeth Feiner's head rolled off the pillow and on to the wooden bedstead. Underneath the pillow, on a sheet grey with mould, lay the gaudy yellow tin of sardines.

The stench drove Rosemarie Ilse Herz a step back. She stared at the tin and, her hand pressed against her mouth, she gave a slight scream. Looking at the sardines, carefully wrapped and giving the impression of plenitude, she grew suddenly furious.

'Well, and then we think that they're dying of hunger!' she exclaimed.

'The swine!' said Herta by way of an answer.

She leant towards Rex and, her voice quiet and inciting, urged the dog: 'Go on, fetch! Fetch, Rex!'

The animal bounded forward and in one leap reached Elizabeth Feiner's bedside. She was not aware of its presence. Her eyes were already closed. She no longer knew whether anyone was standing next to her, how far away they were, nor if there was anyone in the room at all. She only felt the dog's hot breath on her face, but did not see its open mouth.

All this time Werner Binde had been standing quite still, and it seemed that his eyes penetrated everything with their glassy stare, encompassing everything with a single, greenish-grey look. Suddenly he came alive – before either of the two women realized what was happening he had a pistol in his hand and fired.

There was a hurt, surprised look in the wounded Alsatian's eyes, and the animal gave out a rattling sound. Finally it fell and remained lying motionless across the open suitcase.

Herta cried out.

Then, screaming and holding hands, she and Rosemarie Ilse

Herz ran through the narrow space between the bunks, out on to the veranda, and down the stairs.

Still not a muscle had moved in Werner Binde's flat face. He was still standing where he was, immobile. Then with his usual rolling gait he crossed over to the bunk where only fractions of time divided Elizabeth Feiner from death. But this he did not know. Very gently he moved her head back to the pillow and re-arranged her blanket. The old woman's ugly, angular head suddenly seemed to him tender and kind. At that moment she reminded him of his stepbrother, Fritz. It was then he realized that there was more to it than just his personal duel with Maurice Herz. And although his brain immediately started a feverish search for some means of averting the suspicion which his action was sure to arouse, he was aware of something dark at the bottom of his consciousness that would have to be thought out later. Then he bent down, picked the dead animal up by the legs, and, with a single jerk, slung it across his shoulders. Then he waddled out of the room and down the stairs to the car.

'Oh, Herr Binde, what happened?' Rosemarie Ilse's teeth chattered as she spoke.

'Why did you do it?' asked Herta, nervously smoothing her hair under its broad red band.

Werner Binde measured them with his fish-cold eyes, which penetrated Rosemarie Ilse to the marrow of her bones, and before whose stare Herta's eyes swerved away. Then he dumped the dog on the floor of the car.

'Where do we go from here?' he asked, speaking slowly and in a dull voice. After a while, nonchalantly and without deeming it necessary to turn his face towards them, he explained, drawing out the words:

'That dog . . . it was sick . . . I saw it. It had the rabies.'

'Oh . . .' said Rosemarie Ilse.

Herta was silent.

When they got in, Rosemarie Ilse loathingly drew her feet away from the dead animal.

Binde turned the car round, and then drove along the main

L Avenue, along damp mounds of russet-coloured leaves, past the shuttered shop underneath the stone sun, and back to the German H.Q.

8

Two beautiful sleek limousines stood outside the white house which flew the swastikas on its flagstaffs. They were not painted the dull grey military colour, but, on the contrary, shone blackly like dark mirrors. Each car had a little flag on the radiator, the red cross standing out against the white background.

A clean-shaven, slim gentleman in a 'pepper-and-salt' suit of perfect cut turned – evidently in the name of all the other gentlemen – to Albert Heinz Ritsche, the commandant of the Large Fortress of Terezín, for there was no time left to see the Small Fortress, and said:

'What we have seen so far, Herr Kommandant, is enough for the time being, really. We have a long journey ahead of us.'

'Quite, I understand,' replied Ritsche politely, without trying by as much as a hint of insistence to prevail upon them to remain longer. 'At your service, gentlemen.'

The company then slowly climbed into the cars and drove off to the accompaniment of general hand-waving.

The officers from the H.Q. who had accompanied the guests walked unhurriedly back into the building.

Werner Binde stopped his car just as the second shining limousine disappeared behind a bend in the road.

Maurice Herz turned round when he heard the sound of the car's brakes, and saw his wife Rosemarie Ilse, Herta, and the driver. He went back to meet them.

'What a coincidence we didn't meet,' he said. 'We were in the ghetto with them a few moments ago.'

Werner Binde muttered something under his breath. Then he lowered his eyes, excused himself, and got back into the car.

He drove at once to a valley between two villages near the town, and threw the dead dog out on to the rubbish-heap.

9

About three weeks after the morning on which the Swiss health committee paid its visit to the Jewish ghetto in Bohemia, Werner Binde again drove Rosemarie Ilse Herz to town. This time Maurice Herz was with them, his wife having asked him to accompany her.

Rosemarie Ilse started her work of requisitioning in exactly the same way as she had done twenty-one days ago – from Room 38. Werner Binde noticed that in the very corner, underneath the barred window where Elizabeth Feiner had lain, there was an empty bunk.

And then, on their way back, even though they drove very rapidly along L Avenue, he saw quite clearly that the customers in the shop known as 'The Sun' were being served by a strange man with his hat worn low on his forehead, and a black-haired girl.

The Children

VICKY stamped his feet impatiently.

If only Jacob were back, he thought, they could go out for a while. Time passed so slowly, they had the whole day in front of them yet. Maybe they'd see a white horse – that meant luck. Or they could slip through into the baths. Or climb a tree on the East Rampart, right up on to the 'monkey branch', and have a good swing in the wind.

From the courtyard a few feet away he could hear a wailing noise – that was Fifka killing a cat. He was standing in the open space between two door posts where a door once used to to be, was holding the cat by the tail and swinging it from side to side, each time knocking its head against the wooden threshold. This had been going on for some half an hour already. Occasionally Vicky would overhear a muttered word or two: 'Go on, die, you bugger!' It was a three-coloured cat, most probably the only one in the whole ghetto. The boys would roast it like a hare.

At last there was a triumphant shout from Fifka.

And then silence.

Vicky was standing on a wet red brick and a wide puddle glistened underneath. On top, the baked clay displayed a fan-shaped motley of reddish hues. It was slowly crumbling away, piece by piece, with each stamp of Vicky's feet.

The breeze ruffled the surface of the puddle, the turbid water mirroring Vicky's frail body and face in small, jerky waves.

What now? Vicky's left shoe gaped open at the front, and small, dirty toes protruded from the yawning leather. He gazed at them helplessly. He lifted his big toe – it stuck out

over the puddle like a big cannon. The brick would certainly
fall to pieces. He could only save himself by jumping immediately on to dry land. But still he hesitated: the shoe and
his toes would suffer.

Helplessly he wiped his nose on his sleeve.

What a bloody fool, he reviled himself, to mooch about
here on a brick in the water. It was all because of that silly
waiting! Jacob had been down already, but Ginger had sent
him back to sweep the corridor. Ginger was the worst of all
the prefects in Home Q 719. He was sure to meet with an accident one of these days and they all hoped he would. Vicky too.
Only Vicky could not afford to ignore him like Fifka did.
Fifka was a 'half-caste', his mother was a Jewess, at present
somewhere in Poland, and his father a German, racially
absolutely pure! Of whom it was even said that he was in the
SS, only no one knew that for certain and Fifka did not speak
about it. Once, however, he had said that he was going to kill
his father after the war. He took no notice of anything or anybody, and they, Vicky and Jacob, would one day be exactly
like him. Ginger would get what he deserved, with interest, he
needn't think he wouldn't – he would get it right on the snout.

Vicky's little face with its slightly upturned nose suddenly
beamed. That was it!

He pulled a piece of string out of his pocket. Casting an ex-
pert glance at his toes to see if the mud had dried sufficiently,
he bent forward and began to tie the shoe together with large,
thorough knots, from time to time balancing himself stork-
wise on one leg. At last the loose, flapping sole was again
fastened to the worn upper, with only a few rusty nails stick-
ing out. This, however, did not bother him.

He poised himself for the jump and then leaped across.
The last remaining piece of brick slowly submerged in the
puddle.

'Victor!'

Taken by surprise, Vicky looked up. It was Berl, Ginger's
assistant. He recognized the voice even before his eyes took
in the thin, narrow face, the bulging green eyes, and the in-

gratiating half-smile which Berl wore in the corner of his
mouth and which he never took off.

'What're you jumping about down there for like a goat?' he
called down to Vicky. 'I bet you haven't even reported for
fatigue today, have you?'

'Sure I have!' replied Vicky. 'I have been going out to the
Kavalírka for over a week now to dig the ditch for the fence,
remember?'

The prefect carefully scrutinized Vicky's cheeky face and
then withdrew his large-eyed head.

There! Vicky thumbed an imaginary nose at him. Berl, as
Vicky well knew, was today taking the boys from dormitories
16 and 20 to work at felling trees. Yesterday, already, they had
been looking for children to go on this work party. Vicky
glanced down at the toes of his shoes, wondering whether the
left one would survive if he gave Berl a kick in the pants to
take, at least for a moment, that silly grin off his face. True,
Berl was a degree or two better than Ginger, there was no
denying that. But Vicky had only to remember that Berl was
just as stuck-up as Ginger, exacting the same show of defer-
ence and the same respectful saluting from the boys, and he
was heartily sick of him. Still, he would never have expected
Berl to fall so easily for his yarn about the Kavalírka – Vicky
had not been there for the third day running now.

Thinking it better to play safe, Vicky at once shambled off
into a corner, so that in case of emergency he could hop over
the wall. Fifka was probably gone by now; they were most
likely in some dry place, skinning the greyish-black cat with
the white spots. Now he understood why Fifka had brought
home that rusty old frying-pan last night.

It sure took a long time, pondered Vicky, to bash in such a
small creature's head.

It looked like rain.

This puddle which had swallowed up the brick – Vicky
thought, following a new idea – had been there for over a week.
And it would become deeper still. Everything, every blessed
thing here seemed so sleepy, the courtyard, too, and the walls,

and the image of the cat's skin without the animal inside it.
Oh, Vicky – he said to himself as he stretched himself and
spread out his arms like wings – the things that happen in this
world.

Above Vicky's brown, curly head, capless in every weather,
swam light-grey clusters of cloud. Vicky's grey eyes merged
with their shadows and followed them attentively as they were
driven by the wind above the town and beyond. Vicky could
read of unattainable things in them: the rock behind Terezín,
out of which they were just then taking a bite, was like a big
ship which was sailing into the blue. No, Vicky corrected himself, the ship was standing still, only a sea of wind and clouds
went drifting past and the waves were receding.

Vicky wrinkled his freckled forehead gloomily. It looked
even smaller than it really was, owing to the ringlets of hair
that grew practically out of its middle. He felt sad that he had
to stay behind while the sky sailed on into a different world.
Then the unseen hand which had shaded his face suddenly
vanished. Vicky – a dreamy voice seemed to be saying somewhere inside him – oh Vicky, if only you could stand right up
there and look down from that height on to the ghetto and
spit right in the middle, on the church spire in the square. Or
at least if you could come to the baker's shop on Q Street and
the baker had left the ventilator gates open. Imagine, running
over to Fifka tomorrow and throwing a loaf of bread on his
bunk! Would he be surprised! Just like Jacob was when he,
Vicky, had nosed out that ventilator despite the fact that so
many hungry people came walking past 813 on Q Street every
day! But – a warning voice cautioned Vicky – what if Fifka
pinched the bread and polished off the cat's meat by himself
just the same. He wouldn't put it past him – that was just the
kind of thing Fifka might do.

In his mind's eye Vicky returned to Q Street, where he had
discovered a possible entrance to the bread kingdom. The
spaces between the steel vanes of the ventilator were extremely
narrow, but with his snake-like body he could get in and Jacob
could keep watch outside. In a few weeks' time it might be too

late, because they were growing! But, Vicky consoled himself, they would do it, sometime. Sure they would. Sometime in the evening. Or at night. Now – he stuck his hands in his pockets, thoroughly disgusted – now it was cold and it was day. And it was no good in the daytime.

Vicky looked down at his shoes again: a pair of dilapidated soles, mud all the way up to his ankles, and a bandage of string on the left. He stopped kicking with the toe of one foot against the heel of the other and started to rock on his heels instead, his hands deep in his pockets, right up to his blue wrists. What the hell, he thought, unable to shake off the idea, what if he and Jacob really did get in there!

He stared at the sky. It was so pleasant thinking about it. If they were lucky and the thing came off, he would go straight away the next morning and give his share to Helen. She would open her small mouth in surprise, just as she had done that time when he had climbed down the rampart, with its many holes and projections, into the commandant's garden and brought her a velvety yellow rose. 'Vicky,' she had said, 'you are a right boy, after all.' He had not been afraid to do it, although Fifka, when he got to know about it, had voiced his opinion that *he* would not dream of troubling himself on account of such a Princess Wet-her-pants. And Helen had told him that she would go out for a walk with him, if he wished.

Vicky did not feel the chillness of the wind. Perhaps one day, he day-dreamed, Helen would be his girl. Really his girl, with all that goes with it. At least she would not then be so thin and sickly all the time. Vicky would get her everything she needed. Even meat – perhaps.

Lost in thought, Vicky now completely stopped taking any notice of what went on in the courtyard. Before his eyes he had a soft rose, composed of thin, firm petals which opened of their own accord. There existed such gentle and fragile things like the back of a small house or a rose, it occurred to him, and yet at the same time it seemed somehow incredible that they should exist.

Leading the party of boys from dormitories 16 and 20, Berl

passed through the courtyard and out of the gate, those in
the rear clinking their axes. 'Quiet there, you rotters!' shouted
Berl. But in the next instant he grinned at them to show them
that he was not such a bad fellow, after all. The boys' voices
cascaded down the staircase into the yard like a sudden storm,
only to die away again immediately afterwards as the strong
wind wafted them away.

Vicky was oblivious of his surroundings. He relived again
that moment when, holding the rose in his fingers, he had felt
an overpowering urge to say something nice to Helen, or to
stroke her. He had wanted to say a whole sentence composed
of a lot of nice words – and then he had not said a word. He
had not even taken her hand as he had intended. Helen kept
coughing all the time because she had on only a thin dress. In
the end she had taken the rose and had run off home with it.
There had been no walk, nothing. All that Vicky saw had
been the empty street, the cobbles and the doorways of the
houses, so stupidly similar; along the whole of Q Street
nothing but barracks and houses, barracks and houses.

The cold buffeting wind at last brought Vicky back out of
his dream world in which reigned the undernourished Helen
from the Difficult Children's Home where they had refused to
accept Fifka for fear that he would spoil the other children,
Helen, the little girl with the nervous light-blue eyes and the
long, straw-coloured hair falling down on to her shoulders.

It was better to think of the ventilator. After that day, Helen
had not been allowed out for quite a time, but he was sure that
it was not because she wetted herself, as Fifka had said. No, it
was no use trying that thing with the ventilator in the daytime.
Not in the daytime.

The knots on his shoe came undone.

He crossed the courtyard once more, right to the other side
near the passage, in order not to stand about in one place and
thus give Ginger a chance of grabbing him and sending him
out to work after all. He also had to do something about that
shoe of his to keep his toes from getting wet.

Just then Jacob appeared at the top of the staircase. Taking three steps at a time, he came leaping and bounding down in a flash.

'Hi ya, Vicky!'

'Hi ya!' said Vicky. 'About time!'

'Come on, quick!' replied Jacob, without stopping. 'I've got to get out.'

They raced through the passageway and out into the stony embrace of the street and the pavement, the embrace of freedom.

'That bloody ginger rat,' said Jacob as soon as they were round the corner. 'I hope he croaks soon, Vicky.' And a while later, as Vicky did not respond: 'If only they put him in the first transport to go from here.'

'Who, Ginger?'

That, of course, was a purely rhetorical question.

Vicky stopped and took his shoe off.

'Wait a minute. I've got to fix this,' he said by way of an explanation.

Jacob handed him a stone.

'Thanks.'

'That's a lovely hole,' said Jacob, looking on with interest as Vicky hammered the nails into their original holes.

Vicky straightened himself up. 'Done,' he said.

'He made me clean practically the whole house,' said Jacob.

'I was beginning to think that he had collared you for the day,' said Vicky, throwing a disdainful backward glance.

'He wanted some more chaps to go felling trees, you understand.'

'Sure,' said Vicky. 'I guess that's why Berl called out to me whether I had been detailed for work.'

'To hell with the lot of them,' said Jacob.

'We'll make them pay for it one day, Jacob, you see if we don't.'

Jacob nodded.

One day – they were both thinking – that meant in a year or two when they had grown out of their unsatisfactory children's size.

'What it needs is just a good pair of fists, that's all,' said Jacob.

A pause.

But they understood one another very well.

Vicky scanned the passers-by with his eyes, while Jacob's roved higher up, along the cornices and windows. On the other side of the street a Jewish policeman was pacing his beat in a waterproof and with a yellow-black cap on his head. In the window above him stood a bottle of thin, bluish milk. The baby ration.

Jacob winked at Vicky.

'Vicky!'

They both looked up.

'I guess we could pinch that,' suggested Vicky.

'That's right, we could,' said Jacob. 'But not now – in the evening.'

'But it won't be there any more in the evening,' said Vicky.

'All right, let's forget the bottle, then,' said Jacob. 'It probably belongs to some sick little kid anyway.'

'Sure thing, Jacob,' said Vicky.

The policeman turned towards them and they were careful not to let their eyes stray to the window with the bottle in it any longer.

We noticed it, that's the main thing, the expression on Jacob's face seemed to say, while Vicky thought: 'We miss nothing in this dump – last week the ventilator and now the milk!'

Jacob started to spit and Vicky to whistle.

The policeman went on and only the two of them knew what he had missed, walking past without an inkling as to what was going on here. He wore a small moustache and he reminded Jacob of a beetle. 'Looks like a ruddy beetle,' Jacob thought.

Jacob lifted his face and, sniffing at the wind, he snorted, expertly smelling the scents and odours of the town.

They had reached the corner between Q and L street.

'Gosh, Vicky, look!'

A flat-bottomed cart was coming towards them. Vicky had turned because the man they had just passed had somehow reminded him of his father, though he at once discarded the idea as downright silly, for no one knew where his father had got to. And so it happened that he all but ran smack into the flat-bottomed cart of the bakery.

'Gosh!' he said softly, stunned, as Jacob had been before him, by the sight of the loaves of bread neatly stacked in oval, yellow pyramids. It was as though countless bells had begun to chime somewhere inside him, all of them at once. Well, well, the street was offering the young gentlemen breakfast on its stone platter.

Jacob distended his nostrils and snorted like a horse. He looked so funny that Vicky almost laughed. How comically he doubled himself up and stuck out his belly!

Jacob felt the blood going to his head. What a stroke of luck, he thought, and first thing in the morning, too!

'Where do we start, Vicky boy?' he asked with a drawl. 'Would you care for the bottom ones or would you prefer those at the top?'

'Gosh!' repeated Vicky. 'Aren't we lucky!'

The cart passed by. Jacob crossed over to the opposite pavement. Now they were all set for a nice pincer movement. They winked at each other. Vicky kept taking deep breaths of the provocative, intoxicating smell. Holding back a little, they walked on inconspicuously behind the cart. Naturally the first thing they had to do was to find out from where this fragrant treasure came and where it was being taken.

The cart rattled and rocked over the cobbles. It was pulled by a dozen men, the only horse in the ghetto having fallen ill.

Vicky, his grey eyes shining, smiled in Jacob's direction every now and then. They were in luck, after all, he thought, although Jacob's morning encounter with Ginger and his own with Berl had not been exactly a good omen. A warm wave flooded Vicky's body. He would have liked to do something, to jump to the cart, simply pick up a loaf, and beat it. But that was impossible. They would do it some other way, he did not

know how yet, but they would, he told himself and again felt
that rising wave of satisfaction inside. They were too smart for
Berl and Ginger! They would not go and slave away for them
at the Kavalírka, and as for Ginger's and Berl's high faluting
ideals, all about the Promised Land in return for sweet-sound-
ing promises and half a meal extra, they could keep those as
well! Jacob and he would get their extras elsewhere. Right
here, he thought, looking at the cart as it rattled on its way.
And then, in a year of two, they would step out along the main
L Avenue, handsome and debonair, Vicky with Helen on
his arm – and Helen with a genuine alligator handbag under
hers! – everybody they met would turn to look at them and to
whisper approvingly: 'That fellow with the beautiful girl,
that's Vicky, and the other one is his faithful pal, Jacob.'

At long last the flat-bottomed cart stopped.

Impatient now, Jacob ran across to Vicky, again distended
his nostrils and snorted in Vicky's ear. Vicky gurgled with
laughter. No sooner had Jacob glanced at the front of the
house, however, than something seemed to snap inside him;
he stopped short and turned pale, his nose narrowed and his
mouth fell at the corners. Vicky saw him direct a surreptitious
look towards the sultry sky and then cast his eyes down as if
they wished to pierce the pavement.

'What's up?' asked Vicky.

'Nothing,' replied Jacob. 'Why?'

'Look, Jakie, you stay here and watch where they put the
bread, an' I'll go and find out where they loaded it.'

'And then you'll come back here?'

'Well, sure . . .'

'Vicky,' Jacob interrupted him suddenly, 'look at that
house.'

'What for?'

'That's the house . . .'

'What house?'

His curiosity aroused, Vicky looked carefully at the cracked
plaster of the shabby house in front of them. Wasn't it perhaps
. . . Yes, that was it. Now he knew.

Something went dead inside him. Willy-nilly he had to re-
call something that had not been really forgotten in any case.
It had merely been pushed down somewhere to the bottom of
his consciousness and kept there, safely tucked away, by the
simple expedient of piling every little thing that each day
brought on top of it. It had weighed heavily on his mind at
the time, and now it all came back with a rush. It came so
terribly quickly, thought Vicky, so suddenly and so vividly
that he saw himself and Jacob, as they were that time, climb-
ing up on to that ledge and gesticulating wildly to frighten the
inhabitants in the windows just above. Vicky was carried back
to that day when their walk along the narrow ledge had given
them an insight into rooms such as they had never seen before.
The house in front of which they were now again standing
was a home for the aged, and in it they had that other time
seen old women with faces like parchment and with ugly,
wrinkled skin on their throats, old women who would probably also be there today. And in a dusky corner which stank
of rotting straw and ammonia there knelt an old woman.
Vicky again saw her in front of him and again felt the same
sickly wave of revulsion. Her body was yellow and it was
swathed in dirty bandages. Jacob had snorted and they had
all started with fright. Somebody had cried out. There was
something in the old woman's eyes which had scared them
both, but Jacob recovered straightaway. 'Look,' he had told
Vicky, ashamed of his momentary feeling of compassion. He
had pulled out of his pocket a piece of bread originally intended to augment their lunch. Vicky had looked at the bread
and said: 'What do you want to do with it?' And Jacob, quite
cheerful again, had added: 'Just watch!' and flung the crust
at the old hag in the corner. It must have been quite a force-
ful blow, because – this, in particular, came back to Vicky
very clearly now – the old woman had clutched at her side and
had fallen to the floor with a gasp. Vicky felt a twinge at his
heart. All the old woman's pain stared at Vicky out of her
eyes which were looking directly at him. Shocked, he had let
go of the window and only just in time managed to catch hold

of a projection on the window sill. Something was impelling him towards those eyes, making him want to climb inside and stroke the old woman's hair in spite of her filthiness and his abhorrence. Perhaps the fact that she had derived no benefit from that crust of bread, which had been snapped up by the others, also had something to do with it. But he refrained, held back by his loathing, which not even the aged eyes, empty and extinct and – that most of all! – reproachful, were able to overcome. He hardly knew how he had succeeded in getting down from the ledge, those two eyes staring at him out of every brick and every blemish in the plaster.

'That's right, Jacob,' he repeated now. 'That's the house.'

So this was where the bread was being taken.

The two boys stood a little distance away, silent, and without even looking at one another.

The bread was quickly unloaded from the cart.

But Vicky no longer cared.

There was a dead silence now. Everything pleasant that Vicky had felt as a result of his hope, personified by the shape and smell of the loaves, had gone.

As for Jacob, to judge by his appearance, he was feeling physically sick, standing there pale and with his mouth half open, staring at the empty cart which used to be a funeral wagon before the wooden construction had been taken off so that it could serve for the noon delivery of bread; its bare and worn wooden boards, over which thin veils of mist were now swirling, were like an open book containing the single dreary word – disillusion.

So they stood, Vicky and Jacob, sad and downcast side by side.

It occurred to Vicky that it was up to him today to be the first to recover and thus to even up the score with Jacob. And anyway, he thought, all was not lost yet. After all, they did not necessarily need just *these* loaves. At last he glanced at Jacob. His long face with the almost transparent nose seemed to be saying: don't kid yourself, Vicky. But why were they standing here for such a long time? And what had happened to the chaps who pulled the cart?

They appeared a few moments later, followed by a group of old men.

Vicky strained his eyes. What was it they were carrying in that white sheet? Then, suddenly, he knew: it was a corpse. Vicky again glanced at Jacob, whose face now bore a striking resemblance to a sheat-fish with its drooping mouth; for Jacob, too, had just realized what the white sheet concealed. Vicky's eyes again turned in that direction. Strands of grey hair fell loosely from the two planks and white coverlet. It was a woman.

Jacob spat.

It flashed across Vicky's mind that this was perhaps the old woman at whom Jacob had thrown the bread. And again the whole scene came back to him as it had a while ago. It was disconcerting, the source of something that killed all hope in Vicky's heart, hope that gleamed like the smooth cobbles over which the day went gliding from morning till sunset until they were drowned in the dark pool of night. Vicky grimaced. He was thinking of the sore-encircled eyes of the yellow-skinned old woman who did not even have a chemise. But he remained silent. What was there for him to do, anyway? There was a catch in his throat, and he would have dearly liked to speak and to hear Jacob say something. However, it was perhaps just as well that they could just stand there in silence, without having to speak.

The cart moved forward.

Vicky did not like the look of the old men who walked behind it. The dead woman's husband, dressed in an old coat, carried his head high in a vain attempt to lend a little dignity to their journey.

Vicky trailed behind, until Jacob turned and asked: 'What's the matter with you, chum?' Immediately, however, he remembered that it was Vicky who had asked him a similar question not so long ago.

'It's no use, Jacob,' said Vicky.

Jacob spat in a graceful arc into the ditch.

'I could have told you that ages ago,' he said.

Yet they walked on.

Is it her? Vicky was asking himself. What kind of hair did she have that time? Those eyes of hers won't be looking like that any more, then. When you died you just didn't look at anything any more and you didn't think of anything. You were through. And you were at peace! At least, that's what people said. Why was he thinking about it, though, it was just plain silly to think about it. But what if she did die and had never recovered from that blow? Go on, he told himself, that blow could not have been as strong as all that. It could not have been so strong! The thought was immediately followed by a conflicting one: was it really so strong for such an ailing and emaciated body?

They had reached the barrier. Halt! The end of the ghetto.

The cart went on, only the small procession accompanying it remained behind.

Vicky caught up with Jacob, and together they stood looking out after the cart until it disappeared behind a bend in the road. A little calmer and more composed, Vicky reflected that now they would never know whether it had been she or not.

'Jacob,' he said, 'I guess the cart won't come back for bread any more today.'

'Well, shall we go, then?'

'Yes, let's. Come on!'

'Sure, I'm coming,' said Jacob, but he remained where he was.

'All right, I guess we'd better let them pass first . . .' added Vicky.

The old men were coming back. Terezín was welcoming them with the damp, icy breath of its brick-and-mortar lungs.

Now and again Vicky would scan the horizon. The high rock beyond the town was, after all, a ship sailing for some other world. The summit of the rock – that was the ship's prow – was cleaving its way through limitless space, lined at the start by the hill and copse and then by nothing at all. 'I wonder if anyone can guess what is over there where you can't see from here,' thought Vicky.

He looked at Jacob. What would he do if they were not such good friends? Vicky felt a sudden upsurge of affection for Jacob, and he ran his eyes swiftly over his face, the small forehead, thin little nose and mouth that droops whenever he is annoyed about something, as he was just now. Then Vicky's eyes roamed upwards again.

'What do you keep staring at the hills for?' Jacob asked.

Vicky did not reply.

'Come on, walk faster, can't you. The wind is such a nuisance.'

'We'll catch cold,' thought Jacob angrily.

They went on like this, side by side. His casual glances at the countryside filled Vicky's soul with something that was strange and a little inaccessible at the same time, making him feel slightly afraid. He put his arm around Jacob's shoulders and pressed himself close to him.

'I am quite cold,' he said.

'Well, you needn't think you're making me any warmer,' retorted Jacob. Nevertheless, he clung to Vicky, too.

At last they were in the town.

They did not feel like talking, so they just wandered about in silence. Jacob no longer sniffed the air, seeing that things had turned out the way they did. They passed barracks with the high-sounding names of Dresden and Hamburg, towns which the two boys had never seen, walked past the de-lousing station, across the square with the church, underneath which it was said there were secret underground passages, and along by the coal yards.

I wish Jakie would snort like a horse again, Vicky said to himself. He did not want to ask him to do it, however, as that struck him as rather silly. Occasionally it seemed to Vicky that Terezín was a huge town, but that was only an illusion which sprang from the fact that it was so badly overcrowded. He did not mind that, though. What mattered now and what made him uneasy was that things had gone wrong right from the start today, beginning with Ginger and Berl. And that cart should not have gone to that silly house. What if it *was* the old woman, after all? The houses and the whole town seemed to him to be swathed in dirty bandages. Terezín was a woman, no chemise and her body one big sore. Even the passers-by seemed to have caught the infection, and Vicky tried to find out, by means of surreptitious, but at the same time penetrating glances, whether their clothes did not hide the festering blue spots of impetigo.

A few steps ahead, Jacob was walking on with a rolling gait, giving Vicky the opportunity of observing his ankles, purple with cold, as Jacob had exchanged his socks for two ounces of sugar. Despite the cold, Jacob was pleased that his trousers had become too short for him owing to his rapid growth. Now he was walking serenely on, hands in his pockets. his nose a red blotch in a pallid face, and his scarf around his neck, spitting to right and left as he went. From time to time he stopped and turned his head nonchalantly to look back over his shoulder without turning his body. He waited for Vicky, watching his gaping shoe as he did so. Jacob had by now come to the conclusion that it was all not the slightest bit of use, and his head was full of this idea. If it weren't for his mother, he would be out of the ghetto by tomorrow. They'd go some place with Vicky. As it was, there was nothing they could do but go and fetch their lunch and stop by to see his mother towards evening so that she should not be worried about him. Everything was black, black as pitch. Jacob stopped again and the pupils of his eyes encountered the grey eyes of his friend.

'Vicky,' he said suddenly, 'maybe it won't be so horrid here in summer, will it?'

Vicky stared at him questioningly, but said nothing.

'Maybe it won't, Jacob,' he said finally, after a while. 'There are flowers here – and sometimes even fruit.'

They started on a second trip round the town, Vicky, in his chequered blouse, by this time almost as cold as Jacob, an absent look in his grey eyes. In them was imprisoned his dream of Helen with the alligator handbag. And the other one of the grown Vicky, handsome and strong, well-dressed and enjoying Jacob's friendship.

Jacob was walking at his side, his skull numb with the frost and with the nagging question of what he was to bring his mother by way of an extra for her supper without having to barter his scarf. Every now and again he would hop on one leg and warm his ankles with the palms of his hands.

'Jacob,' said Vicky.

'What?'

'What do you think the woman in that house died of?' He had actually wanted to ask something quite different – if it had not occurred to Jacob too that it might be the same old woman he had wanted to give the piece of bread to that time – but this question slipped out instead.

'How should I know, Vicky?' Jacob looked at him. 'Nobody told me, did they?'

'I only asked, Jacob,' said Vicky.

He smiled happily. If Jacob did not know, either, there was no need for him to worry about it.

'I must say, Vicky,' said Jacob, 'you have daft ideas sometimes.'

Of course, said Vicky to himself, Jacob did not even think of it. It did not occur to him because those eyes had not haunted him as they had haunted Vicky. I shan't think about it any more – he promised himself – after all, it needn't have been her at all.

They climbed the steps up to the Eastern Rampart.

Vicky was suddenly overcome with joy. He started to run, leaping over puddles and stamping in some of them until the water and the mud squirted up into the air. He ran to a tree in the corner, then swarmed up it all the way to the 'monkey branch' and even higher, right up to the top.

'Don't be silly!' Jacob called out to him.

And now Vicky caught sight of Helen, who was walking along the edge of the rampart with Fifka. No doubt he had bragged to her how he had killed the cat, it occurred to Vicky.

H

Perhaps he had even invited her to join him in eating the meat. Vicky put his fingers in his mouth and gave a sharp whistle. Then he started to swing on the branch. He still had that feeling of having been relieved of a great burden which Jacob had given him. Who else if not Jacob would have known if it had been her?

He swung a little harder and occasionally glanced in Fifka's direction.

'Vicky!' came Jacob's voice from below. 'Have you gone crazy or what?'

What was Helen thinking just now? There, now she was looking his way. Vicky set the whole tree swinging and clambered on to the thinnest branch of all.

It gave suddenly and violently. Vicky's frail little body spun like a corkscrew – twice he hit projecting parts of the trunk and the branches, the last of which caught in his blouse and ripped it right down to the double-stitched waist-band. Then he plonked down like a dead weight into the wet grass.

It began to rain.

Jacob's heart gave a bound. He stood where he was, helplessly rooted to the spot, his shirt open at the neck and his scarf loose, feeling nothing but the paralysing contraction in his throat.

'Vicky,' he managed to say at last.

Deathly pale, Vicky opened his eyes.

'Am I hurt, Jacob?'

Then he isn't dead, it flashed across Jacob's mind. It was as though something had flared into light inside him. He sprang towards Vicky and slowly raised him up.

Fifka and Helen had arrived by this time. With all three supporting him, Vicky got painfully to his feet.

'By God, you are damned lucky, titch,' said Fifka; then to Helen, 'all right, come on, he'll manage now.'

'Lucky,' whispered Vicky.

The town was slowly becoming engulfed by the mud.

Moral Education

It always took Charlie a long time to go to sleep.

Before sleep finally claimed him he experienced a fleeting feeling of friendship and of pride at the fact that he had been allowed to join the select circle of boys in Room 16. Even in this semi-dormant state he could make out the individual voices in the conglomeration of sounds and smells that filled the room, each of them awakening admiring images in his brain.

Room 16 buzzed with noise. It was a spacious room, filled with three-storey bunks, some of them fat, others gaunt, with ladders at their sides and narrow spaces between them. Charlie was lying right at the top in the corner, without a blanket, listening.

Thomas Knapp, known for short as Handsome, called out to Danny Hirsch:

'I say, have you finished *The Eighteen Carat Virgin*?'

'Not yet. But you know what? I'll buy it off you.'

'Look, Danny . . .'

'You can have my lunches for a week. Here, take the coupons!'

'Look, Danny, I can get you something similar – it's by Pitigrilli, too . . .'

'My lunches for a week. I'll go without. Well, is it a deal?'

'Oh, all right, then.'

Sitting up erect on his bunk, Danny again riveted all Charlie's attention to himself. How wonderful it must be to be able to make such an offer! Danny's figure seemed to grow in front of his eyes. He could see what an immeasurable distance separated Danny from the others. The envy that he felt towards Danny choked him until at last he closed his eyes and conjured up a day-dream in which he saw himself in Danny's

115

place, offering Handsome far more than a mere week of lunches.

Handsome was lying on his stomach, supporting his small, well-combed head in the palms of his hands. He was singing under his breath:

'I'm all alone . . .
Oh, come back to me
Don't let me be
All alone . . .'

He was pleased with himself. He had Danny's lunches for a week. As for *The Eighteen Carat Virgin,* he had read it through three times already, word for word (confidentially, nothing to get excited about!). And he was sure no one would find out that he had torn out all the more interesting pictures. Snore away in peace, he thought.

'Good night, chaps,' he said.

'I'm all alone,
Waiting through the night . . .'

Full of esteem and boundless admiration, which he could not have put into words but which fully consumed him in its ardour, Charlie was softly whispering his good night to the wall.

No one heard him and no one replied. Not even Snow White, the sick boy who slept in the bunk under his.

'Good night, Snow White,' he said again.

'. . . night.'

A quiet, unhealthy voice was wafted up to Charlie, followed immediately by a bout of coughing. When his parents had packed him off from Prague to Terezín, Snow White had already been suffering from a disease for which the thick air of this town could not be good. But it was only for a fraction of a second that Charlie allowed his attention to dwell on Snow White's sickly voice. His entire being clamoured for

some action which would give him the right to take part in
these evening conversations, nonchalant and self-possessed, as
though each and every one of these boys knew his own price,
and on the strength of it weighed even the most insignificant
word he let out into the vapour-filled air of Room 16. He felt
the blood tingle in his veins with the urge to do something,
anything at all, but *something*, an act which the boys would
talk about in connexion with his name before they went to
sleep. With these thoughts Charlie fell asleep in the dense
silence of Room 16, all its vapours and smells floating above
his and Snow White's bunk.

A piercing whistle heralded the morning.

All of them were startled into wakefulness.

Reveille! The prefect entered as soon as the sound of his
whistle died away.

Snow White was coughing, while the twenty-year-old prefect, Schierl, called out:

'Get up, all of you!'

'Snow White can't – don't you see how he coughs?' said
Tony Fetman in a low voice, casting contemptuous glances at
the prefect.

'Morning!' growled Danny.

Then they carried Snow White, still coughing, away to the
infirmary.

'Not a single one of you blighters to remain behind, understand?' said Schierl, looking peremptorily at his watch.

At two minutes past seven he succeeded in driving out even
Oscar Kleiner, who ambled out of the room, a flower in his
buttonhole, the boys' roaring accompanying him all the way
down to the office where they were detailed to work.

Charlie did not move.

He found it hard to believe that Schierl was leaving, thinking that he was the last out of the room, and that he, Charlie,
had actually managed to evade his vigilance and remain behind after reveille. Crouching down on his bunk, he felt a
warm glow of pleasure as the door slammed behind the prefect. But perhaps the only reason they had missed him was

that he did not mean anything around here. They did not even know about his dreams, he thought. Still, he had cause for satisfaction; he had slipped through.

A new, slightly overcast day penetrated into the room through the large, battered windows set in green walls, veiling it in a silence that seemed strange and unnatural. The bunks were drowned in an unusual, all-pervading quiet; from the outside the dust-filled light entered only as a small, timid rectangle between the bedsteads.

The door opened softly.

Charlie lifted himself up cautiously on one elbow. Fetman! What's he want here? he said to himself. Holding his head watchfully raised above the bunk, he could see everything – even the small suitcase which Fetman was pulling out from underneath his bed, the neat compartments inside it, as well as its contents, shiny and glittering: a bottle of Eau de Cologne, shaving kit, and two bluish silk shirts.

Involuntarily, as though the things he was looking down at had wrung from him an ejaculation of astonishment, he gave an unintentional sigh.

Tony Fetman snapped his suitcase shut. He was not alone, it flashed through his head. In a single leap he was at Charlie's side.

'What're you doing here, you rotter?' he gasped.

'Nothing,' whispered Charlie, quickly swallowing a mouthful of saliva that almost made him choke.

'You're nosing about, you scum,' said Fetman.

'I'm not,' replied Charlie, stuttering. 'Honest, Fetty, I . . . I've stayed behind . . . that's all . . .'

'How come? Schierl cleared the place out, so don't tell me you've stayed behind just like that!'

'But I did,' said Charlie. 'I fooled them . . . Schierl I mean . . .'

'He hasn't set you to spy on us, has he?' said Fetman, in a milder tone of voice.

'He doesn't even know me properly,' Charlie replied.

'Come on, climb down!'

Conciliated, Tony Fetman jumped down and returned to his bunk.

If this puny, frightened titch of a Charlie had really pulled a fast one on Schierl, it was not exactly a bad show – for him, that is. On an impulse Fetman produced a packet of biscuits.

'Here,' he said. 'As for this suitcase that you're goggling at, that was sent to me by my aunt. You get my meaning?'

'Sure,' said Charlie, somewhat offended. Then he added: 'Thanks.'

Full of admiration, he bit into his biscuit, gazing into Tony Fetman's mischievous blue eyes.

But Fetman could not bear so much devotion.

'Look here, titch,' he said, 'you needn't look as if I'd saved you from starvation, you know.'

Seeing that Charlie was taken aback by his words, he went on more kindly: 'Maybe we'll take you with us one of these days.'

'Will you really?' asked Charlie.

'You bet. If I say so, then you can bet your life on it.'

Charlie said no more, and Fetman asked him: 'Do you know where Oscar is?'

But that was more than Charlie knew. His eyes roved involuntarily under Oscar's bunk. It had been made up carelessly. Under it was a pair of carefully polished yellow shoes with decorative brass buckles which so perfectly belonged on Oscar Kleiner's feet – and this was, moreover, so widely known – that they were quite safe there.

'If you like,' Fetman said, 'you can come with me right now.'

'Where are you going?' Charlie inquired.

'Come along and you'll find out.'

'O.K. I'll just put my things on. I'll be ready in a jiffy.'

'But get a move on,' said Tony Fetman. 'We've got to beat it out of here. And quick!'

After that he took no more notice of Charlie for a while. He was thinking of where to find Oscar Kleiner. He *must* find him, there was no question about that. With his help, he thought, it will be easier to get rid of that stuff in the suitcase. In his mind he divided off Oscar's share. Oscar was sure to want the box with the shaving tackle, although he had hardly any whiskers to speak of as yet. But that was all right – he deserved it; yesterday he had given him an inconspicuous nod. That had been his part in the business – the rest had been up to Tony himself; a swift leap, a dexterous grab, and a quick getaway. When it came to turning the booty into money, however, there was nobody like Oscar to make a neat job of it!

Charlie was ready to go.

They got out by clambering over a narrow wall. Tony went first, swinging his thin body up with the aid of the lightning-conductor wire.

Now it was Charlie's turn.

He managed it and stood, elated, at Fetman's side. He had the whole day to himself, to be spent with Tony Fetman, free from all supervision by Schierl or by the Valta brothers.

Fetman, however, was annoyed.

'Where has that idiot got to?' he asked for the third time.

Oscar Kleiner was nowhere to be found.

They gave up at last and just walked aimlessly about the town. Tony Fetman told Charlie that every proper fellow in the ghetto had to have a girl – 'the real thing, you know' – before he was fifteen; Charlie stared at him, wide-eyed, reproaching himself for being such a miserable wretch. They were all far, far better than he was. With tears in his eyes he resolved to put into action, at the earliest opportunity and in every detail, all the things that Tony Fetman was telling him about.

At noon he was able to let him have his own lunch; three and a half boiled potatoes and a plateful of watery soup, the entire overture to six hours of hunger until evening, when bread would be doled out to them.

After that they managed to find Oscar Kleiner at last.

He was leaning against the half-rotten beam of the house commonly known as 'Electricians' House'. The attic, far removed from the din and bustle of the town, was the haunt of a select company between thirteen and eighteen years of age.

'Hallo, Oscar!'

He did not seem surprised.

'Hallo yourself, Tony,' he said. 'What's cookin'?'

'Have you got time?'

'That depends,' Oscar said, pointing his chin in Charlie's direction. 'What's this pup doing with you?'

Charlie flushed. Oscar Kleiner was standing there in front of him, spectacles on his nose, his dimpled chin still pointed at Charlie.

'I've brought him along,' Tony Fetman said. 'He's all right.'

'Anything up?' asked Oscar Kleiner.

'Nothing much, Oscar,' Tony said. 'Everything went off without a hitch . . . you can have the shaving bag.'

'That all?'

Tony nodded.

'O.K.'

'Look, Oscar, I've got a couple of shirts, nice silk stuff. Trade them for me, will you?'

'When? Right away?'

'I've been looking for you all day,' said Tony.

'You could have found me here already after lunch. I didn't want to make trouble for Schierl, so I lent a hand with the digging. He was making eyes at me as it was. Look at those rays of sunshine, Tony!'

Charlie, too, had noticed the 'rays of sunshine', as Oscar called them. They were dancing to the muted strains of an accordion – at the moment with Handsome and Danny Hirsch. Diana and Liana, both of them brunettes, were the daughters of a man who until recently had bought up feathers from all over the country, re-selling them in the shape of first-class pillows ('Rival' trade mark) at three times the price. The candles on the beams disappeared in darkness from time to time, giving Charlie the impression that the dancers were moving about in a gloomy halflight. He was breathless with wonder. A different world, he thought. A world that was completely unknown to the other boys in Q House.

'Oscar!' said Tony Fetman challengingly. 'I need it. Will you do it for me or won't you?'

'I dunno,' replied Oscar calmly.

'You don't know, you say?'

Oscar Kleiner was gazing at Tony's lean face, then he glanced briefly down at Charlie. He's found someone else, Oscar thought, but when he needs something, he knows me all right.

'I'll do it for you, Tony. Sure I will,' he said at last.

Tony Fetman smiled. 'Don't put on airs, Oscar.'

'You know where you can go,' said Oscar. 'Shall I take back what I said?'

'All right, then. I've got them ready at home, under the mattress.'

Charlie listened with bated breath.

'Want to stay for a spot of dancing?' Oscar asked. 'Little Bashful here can stay, too,' he added, digging Charlie in the ribs with his elbow.

Charlie gulped, unable to stop himself. He was being invited into this company. God Almighty! Could it be true? Feeling out of place, he looked around. Handsome and Danny Hirsch were standing in the corner, teasing the two girls. Who might all the others be, he wondered. They had not as much as noticed him. They could not all of them be the boys from the electrical workshop, the *élite* of the ghetto. They were boys, Charlie meditated, whom even Schierl and the Valta brothers didn't dare to mess about with!

'I can't dance,' said Tony.

'Nor can I,' whispered Charlie timidly.

'All right, then, beat it,' said Oscar Kleiner. 'I'll scram in a minute, too.'

They filed out of the attic.

Charlie would have liked to turn round, but he did not do so because he was ashamed that he did not know how to speak with girls, nor with Oscar Kleiner.

'Now beat it!' Tony Fetman told him when they were outside. 'I've got something to settle with Oscar.'

He slunk away like a beaten dog.

As he walked off, speechless, with each step he returned in his imagination to the darkened attic. That was it, he reproached himself, he did not know how to dance, nor how to utter a few nonchalant words to the girls. He whispered their names into the darkness: Liana and Diana. Phantoms of grandeur and wealth. Charlie little cared that it was a past grandeur and a vanished wealth. If only he could stand there next to them, all relaxed and unconcerned, like Handsome and Danny Hirsch! He was sick with the realization that it was not like that – and perhaps never would be. All he had to do was to leave and that was the end of it. If he were one of them, he would have tomorrow to look forward to, but as it was there was nothing, nothing at all. Nothing! Nothing! Loneliness, insignificance, futility, disenchantment. He felt as though he had been in a warm place and they had driven him out into the frost.

He wandered about the streets.

Emptiness.

And yet there smouldered in him a faint hope that this day need not be the last after all. The fragrant smell of the lime-trees blossoming on both sides of the street, the open windows, and everything he had experienced a while ago roused a desire to get over it all somehow, to escape this emptiness and frustration, to stand up and shout: Look where I am. Here! And I'm standing pretty firm! Just you try and push me, you mugs! I shan't fall!

In bed that evening Room 16, despite its sad air of gloomy contemplation, seemed to him gay and lively, unostentatious, of its own accord filled with the real feats of the boys, who never talked about them until they were discovered. What a lucky fluke, he thought; had it not been for his chance getaway from Schierl that morning, he would have known nothing about the way Danny Hirsch, Handsome and Oscar Kleiner had spent the afternoon. He would have been that much the poorer now, and he would be tomorrow and after that unless *something* happened. *Something!*

He rolled about on the bunk, listening to the noises in the room. Snow White, back from the infirmary, was coughing. They did not want him in the infirmary and he, unaccustomed to shouting or quarrelling, had obediently brought his bedding back again.

A few moments later Charlie smiled as he intercepted a veiled allusion to Liana and her sister in something that Handsome said to Danny Hirsch. In a flash he forgot all about Snow White. He smiled with them, and suddenly it occurred to him that his excursion with Tony Fetman and the meeting with Oscar Kleiner and the others in the attic of 'Electricians' House', as well as his lucky escape from Schierl which had started it all, the present from Tony, the greater part of which he still had safely stowed away under his pillow, and a glance at Tony Fetman's suitcase ('as for this suitcase that you're goggling at, that was sent to me by my aunt!') – that all this meant the beginning of something that he himself was perhaps going to finish. The snag, however, was how – where to start, when, and with whom. And a thousand other things. Nevertheless, he felt better. And when Tony Fetman threw a cigarette up to him, Charlie saw that he was *in,* and that Oscar Kleiner had succeeded in trading everything. He comprehended the satisfaction of those two down below, as if it had been he who had exchanged the shirts for cigarettes – the most stable currency in the ghetto – and as if he had a perfect right to share the proceeds. Feeling very happy about everything, Charlie turned on his side, put the cigarette, which had been thrown up to him already lighted, between his lips, took a deep pull at it, and started coughing violently.

Just like Snow White, he thought. Snow White . . . shouldn't he offer him a biscuit? Or should he rather keep them all for himself? Snow White never had anything. He took another draw at his cigarette and his head swam. He felt sick. It was no use, he didn't know how to smoke. But never mind, he'd have another try. He started coughing again.

'What's the matter?' Snow White asked him in his quiet voice.

Charlie thought he was going to choke.

'Nothing, Snow White,' he said. 'Why should anything be the matter?'

He would give the kid that biscuit, after all, just to show him that he was somebody.

'Here, Snow White, take this and eat it.'

'What is it?' Snow White asked.

'Go on, take it!' said Charlie, handing him the whole packet. Let the kid see that he knew a thing or two!

He waited for Snow White to ask where he had got them from, so as to be able to say nonchalantly: never you mind, titch!

But Snow White fell to coughing again as he had done in the morning.

Nobody took any notice of him because they were all staring at Handsome, standing with his legs apart in the narrow rectangle between the bunks in the centre of the room and giving an imitation of the Dutch singer, Hannibal van de Hambo, from Amsterdam, trilling up and down the scale:

'Tra – la – lala – lala
tra – la – la . . .'

Danny Hirsch called out to him: 'You sing so beautiful, Handsome – just like Hannibal. But I hope' – here his voice broke as he could not keep back his laughter any longer – 'I hope that he didn't teach you in private lessons!'

Charlie knew, as they all did, that on his walks through the town Hannibal van de Hambo jotted down the names of boys in his notebooks, inviting the best looking ones to his room.

'This has got to be investigated!' Oscar Kleiner shouted from his bunk.

Handsome repulsed their jibes calmly and with assurance.

'Not me,' he said to Danny Hirsch, 'and I don't want to name any names.' Then he added: 'You bleaters – maa-aa-aa . . .'

This was followed by shouts and catcalls from all over the room.

Handsome glanced round the bunks, taking in the storm he had aroused.

'For heaven's sake!' he said. 'You are a lot of kids, that's what you are . . . Well, and what if I *have* been there? Maa-aa-aa . . .!'

He made horns on his head with his fingers, then he put his tongue out at them. 'Maaaa . . .'

'We want to know what he takes – and what he gives,' Danny said, choking with laughter.

Tony Fetman meanwhile stole up to Handsome from behind, and suddenly shouted in his ear: 'Down with your pants!'

Handsome turned round, startled.

Another roar of laughter.

Charlie could hear even Snow White laughing.

'In the first place, don't ruffle my hair,' protested Handsome, smoothing his hair back as he spoke. 'And then . . . well, I got a pound packet of oat flakes out of him.'

'Gosh! I'll be knocking at his door first thing tomorrow. Honest!' shouted Tony Fetman. Then he said: 'What can he ask of a body like this?' and he pulled up his shirt.

'Nothing much,' replied Handsome, looking him over. And then, grinning at all the boys: 'He'll stroke your hair a little, as he did me . . . and, well, your bottom too . . . But nothing more, really, he doesn't want anything more.'

Danny Hirsch sat up on his bunk: 'But, Handsome, you were telling me only this afternoon how he begged you with tears in his eyes to unbutton your pants.'

'Well, so he did,' admitted Handsome. 'But I didn't.'

Nevertheless, they all knew that he had, and more than once.

And Charlie tried to imagine how it had all taken place before Handsome walked away with a big packet of Dutch oat flakes which would provide him with sweet porridge for more than a week. He looked at him with a strange feeling, a mixture of admiration and disgust, of pity and envy, as well as a certain respect for having had the courage to do it. This respect he felt not only for Handsome, but for all the others too.

Tony Fetman was dancing round the room, 'playing' on his own ribs as though they were an accordion and shouting: 'Let him touch my rib!'

A cool breeze was wafted in through the large window, open at the top to let out the assorted smells.

Room 16 slowly went to sleep.

Pity he hadn't kept at least one biscuit, thought Charlie. He hoped that Snow White at least appreciated the fact that he had given them to him. He was sleepy. The breeze lulled him to sleep, the idea that here somewhere there floated a ticket that would admit him to the boys' company gently stroking his forehead; all he had to do was to stretch out his hand and pick it up. This had been the finest day of his life, both the morning and the afternoon, and he would be able to think about it all day tomorrow, and later too. After this there just had to be a way somewhere, and he had to find it.

The building site to which Schierl sent him the next morning was half an hour's walk out of town.

'Take these pickaxes,' the German overseer told them. 'You're not in the ghetto here, and our Führer knows how to reward honest work. You work and you'll see.' Then he left.

All day long Charlie worked on the half-built air-raid shelter by the German hospital, Tony Fetman next to him. Tony swore loudly at each spadeful of earth he threw up. 'Like hell we'll see,' he said at last. 'I'm packing up.'

And he put his spade down and stopped working.

Then they went home.

From that afternoon, remarkable only for Tony Fetman's having thrown away his spade and not budged from the brick on which he had sat down, Charlie's life ran its course, the previous day returning only in memory, a day full of fantasies and facts, the personification of an esteem in which he, too, might share.

The days passed without change.

Except that the next morning, as he got up and climbed down the ladder to the floor, Snow White, always resembling a pale flower, was even paler than usual, his face motionless and as if carved out of blue and white marble.

For a long time Charlie just stood there looking at him, not daring to touch him.

'Fetman!' he said at last. 'Come and take a look at him. He looks queer. Is he asleep . . . ?'

Fetman strolled over slowly, glanced at Charlie, then dropped his eyes to the floor, and very quietly, as though he were forcing himself to speak in his normal tone of voice, he said: 'He's finished . . .'

'Gosh, boys,' said Handsome, frightened, 'you'd better call Schierl.'

Fetman crossed over to his bunk, got a postcard out of his suitcase and, together with Danny Hirsch and Oscar Kleiner, put together a message for Snow White's parents, counting all the time: they already had twenty-eight words and only thirty were allowed.

Schierl arrived.

'Somebody help me carry him,' he demanded.

Tony Fetman volunteered.

Charlie would have liked to help, only he was scared: Snow White was looking so queer. Like a statue.

The two youths carried him out. Nobody mentioned Snow White any more.

That's how it's got to be, thought Charlie. Snow White simply was and now he isn't any longer, because everybody will turn into a statue like he did one day, and in his case it was only to be expected anyway.

Handsome collected Snow White's bedding.

'Look, boys,' he said. 'He's got some biscuits here.'

But nobody took any notice – perhaps they did not want to hear. Only Charlie looked on in silence as Handsome stuffed the biscuits into his pockets.

Snow White's bunk was not to remain empty long – in a short while Schierl brought in another boy to take his place, a boy who looked happy that he had been transferred to Room 16 and did not even insist that the bunk which had been Snow White's should first be remade.

Schierl then had some things to say to various boys, telling Charlie that he was to work permanently on the air-raid shelter.

'Why permanently?' Charlie asked.

'And why not, you lazybones?' Schierl snarled at him.

And Charlie kept quiet. His fate, it now seemed to him, was definitely sealed. He'd be going out every day to dig that shelter until it happened to him as it had to Snow White. He almost wished they would find him like that in the morning, his face like blue marble with white spots.

The days dragged on.

Occasionally Oscar Kleiner or, very rarely, Danny Hirsch took Tony Fetman's place, shovelling up the earth, but none of them were there permanently, until such a time as the air-raid shelter would be finished, as Charlie was. And so he was constantly under the impression that even by going out to dig the boys were following some secret plan of their own which he did not understand. There was some kind of a wall between him and some action in which he had not been invited to participate.

He made up his mind at last: he was going to earn his admission ticket to their company. He must, God Almighty, he simply *must!* Every second he thought about it was torture. On his way to and from work, all the time, with every blow of his pickaxe, which he could hardly hold up, he was thinking it over, trying to think of a way . . .

But how to fool Schierl as he had done that morning?

Schierl was clever. By sending Charlie he was able to keep in the ghetto his favourites, who brought him his meals and probably gave him a share of what they received in their parcels, same as it was said of the Valta brothers.

He would have to invent a really good excuse not to have to go digging.

One morning he went up to Schierl and said brazenly: 'The

I

German overseer doesn't want me there any more, Schierl. He says to send somebody who has better muscles. Otherwise he's going to raise hell, he says, and make our eyes pop out of our heads.'

'How's that?' asked Schierl in surprise.

'I don't know,' lied Charlie, averting his eyes and looking steadfastly at the floor because he was afraid Schierl would see from his face that he was lying.

'Ehm,' said Schierl, uncertain of himself. 'All right, then. I'll send you somewhere else. But don't you run away!'

Charlie stood where he was, jubilant.

But what next? The action he longed for was still immeasurably distant and unreal.

He gazed out of the window. Summer was waning, the fully waxed lime blossoms were falling to the ground in a green shower and the rain was washing them away. And there was autumn already to be felt in the last breath of summer, but not even autumn could waft away from the boys that certain indefinable something that caused Charlie to admire them. If anything, on the contrary. Nothing changed. His visions haunted Charlie wherever he went. Only he himself was so painfully real. He had again got the better of Schierl, and again he did not know what to do. Everything depressed him. He had nothing but his tormenting dreams. And everything both inside and around him was denuded. He felt chilly.

'I can't have you lazing about here,' Schierl told him downstairs in his office. 'You'll go and work on the building site.'

Charlie was detailed to work as a labourer on a building site in the town. It was near the town hall, fortunately in a deserted spot where only a chance passer-by appeared now and then. It was on the left side of the ghetto, near the barracks that housed both the prison and the ghetto administration.

Throughout the first week Charlie maintained a special vigilance, carefully scanning his surroundings. He wondered what might be behind the bars on the top floors, as well as down here where even he could reach. And on the eighth day his great dream suddenly emerged out of the darkness, growing larger with every glance he took at the greyish-black mass of the town hall and the surrounding desolation.

In the evening Schierl was struck by Charlie's appearance: he seemed pleased as Punch about something. What was the matter with the kid? But he paid no attention to it.

I have found my admission ticket among the boys, Charlie kept repeating to himself. I have *found* it! Now he could join Handsome, Danny and Oscar Kleiner as an equal. He had to keep it quiet yet, though. Be patient for a few days. But his time was coming, he thought contentedly. One evening, not too distant now, he would say: boys, come over here. I've brought this for *us*. When he thought about it, however, he could not help trembling. In the evening his thoughts swept along like an avalanche, an endless succession of images without beginning and end, in a vicious circle unrelieved by repose, heralding to him and him alone that his name carried the mark of action, that he had climbed up to the summit of recognition. And once it had happened, once all those in Room 16 knew about it, he thought, it would never be forgotten as long as this lousy town remained a ghetto!

A restless night. Endless deliberation: with whom was he to do it? He came to a sudden decision: those two with whom he had been allowed to go that day when he first felt that he was alive, that afternoon on which he had seen the two girls in the attic of 'Electricians' House'. Yes, that was it – Tony Fetman and Oscar Kleiner.

He'd do it with them.

If only it were morning!

In the morning he stopped Tony Fetman in the wash-room: 'Tony Fetman,' he said. 'I know about something. It's a cinch!'

For the first time he was able to enjoy the effect of his words on Tony's face, just as he had pictured it so many times in the past few days. If everything continued like this, he thought, it would be a great climb up the rope of his imaginings and real action, right among the *élite* of Room 16, a room in which though he lived he did not as yet belong because he had not proved himself in action.

'On the level, Charlie?' asked Fetman.

'Look, you tell Oscar and we'll do it tonight.'

It was too good to be true.

After a talk with both of them, Charlie decided to postpone it by a day. That talk was almost as beautiful as what was in store for them tomorrow.

'But we'll have to get hold of a picklock to get out,' Tony said with a trace of reproach in his voice.

Charlie did not feel at all remorseful. That was probably all as it should be. He could think something up, and he could also make a bloomer, couldn't he. That, after all, was why three of them were going.

'Sure . . .' he said. 'Only I forgot to tell you.'

In the evening the boys in Room 16 fell asleep, weary, the room full of body vapours.

And then the three of them plunged into the womb of advancing night, not stopping until they reached the gate near the town hall, near the house into which they would shortly steal.

The wind soughed in the lime-tree leaves, rain ran along the roofs. Charlie was not afraid; he had mastered his fear on the way. He was now adequately big even in his own eyes.

'Oscar!' he whispered. 'Wipe your specs and chuck a stone into the street opposite.'

They backed away a little.

Oscar picked up a stone and hurled it.

It fell with a ringing sound on the paving stones some way ahead. But that was all, nothing moved anywhere. Charlie was satisfied.

'There's nobody around,' he said.

The only policeman, standing beneath the little wooden shelter by the town hall, was asleep on his feet and, it seemed, had heard nothing.

It was still raining heavily.

'Come on, boys,' said Charlie.

The passage in which the storehouse lay smelled of decay.

Oscar Kleiner, somewhat excited by the thought of this raid put forward by Charlie and Tony Fetman – perhaps the biggest he had ever taken part in – breathed through his mouth so as to keep the stench out of his nostrils. He was glad he had been invited along in spite of the clamouring voices inside him which exhorted him to chuck it while there was still time, to get out of there and go home. After all, he could wait as he usually did when they went raiding with Tony Fetman. The voices were loud and insistent. All at once he felt pains in his stomach. Quickly he crouched down on his haunches on the edge of an empty laundry basket standing in a corner of the passage.

'Hell, what a stink!' said Tony Fetman.

Charlie looked at him. 'Tony,' he said, 'you're going to climb in there alone, aren't you?'

'That's right,' replied Tony.

Here we go, he thought. This was where it really started for him. Not that he was exactly enthusiastic about it, but he felt reluctant to spoil his reputation of a cold-blooded hunter who could keep his head in the thickest of troubles, which was probably how Charlie pictured him. Anyway, he told himself, what was there to fear so far? Everything was exactly as Charlie had described it. The pointed ends of the bars grinned impassably in the darkness. But for us, thought Tony, they will not be impassable! Several of them were shorter than the others and did not reach right up to the ceiling. That was the important discovery Charlie had made. The gap was just big enough to allow Tony to wriggle through. He took hold of the bars and pulled himself up.

'Don't make a sound, you two!' he said, looking down.

At the top he clamped his teeth. Better close his eyes, too, because – it flashed through his head – to get stuck here would be damn unpleasant. He'd say it would!

Then he jumped from four feet up, lithe and silent like a cat.

In the dark of the storeroom he could see tall piles of boxes containing margarine and jars of marmalade.

'Here you are, boys!' he said.

One by one he was rapidly passing the boxes through the bars, not thinking, but working in feverish haste so as to get it over with as soon as possible, like a machine that is revved up to full speed in sight of the finish.

Oscar Kleiner and Charlie piled everything into a sack they had brought with them for the purpose.

'Is it enough?' Tony Fetman pressed himself right up against the bars so that he would not have to shout and could hear their reply.

'What?' whispered Oscar Kleiner.

'Enough,' said Charlie. 'Come on out and we'll scram.'

Carefully, moving like a machine all the time – a jump, a grab with the hands, quick work with the legs – Tony Fetman climbed back over the bars, dragging under his arm another sack, which he had concealed under his shirt and which was now partly filled with small loaves of bread. He'd made it, he thought. He would prove he was no coward even on a show like this.

'Don't be daft, leave it behind!' said Oscar Kleiner.

The sack with the loaves thudded as it fell to the ground on the other side. Tony obeyed Oscar because Oscar knew what was what. And it was no use quarrelling: Tony believed it brought bad luck to the expedition.

'Hurry up!' Charlie urged him.

At last they were together again.

'Pick it up, Oscar,' said Tony.

Charlie picked up one end of the sack without waiting to be told.

But Oscar Kleiner was crouching on the ground again.

'You pig!' said Tony Fetman derisively. 'You stink like an ape.'

Nevertheless, it was all so pleasant and gay in the tense situation that Charlie felt relieved. Tony was trying to be tough, but his voice was high and thin like a child's.

'Ssssh!' hissed Charlie.

Did he imagine it or had he really heard something?

'Stand over by the wall!' he whispered.

They huddled together against the whitewashed vault.

What's up, wondered Oscar Kleiner, buttoning up his trousers.

Upstairs, a lamp flashed its yellow ray.

Horror took hold of all three. Had someone heard them?

Charlie pulled a pair of pliers out of his pocket, heavy black-smith's pliers.

Someone was coming down. There was no doubt about it now. They could hear the footfalls.

A hot wave took the place of the first chill of terror. Charlie grew pale.

Oscar Kleiner was seized by stomach cramps. A moment longer and he would have to let go . . . Quickly he unbuttoned his trousers again.

It might be better to leave everything behind and clear out out of here, thought Tony Fetman. But all of them knew that they must not budge, for there was the policeman outside the town hall.

Take it easy! Charlie commanded himself. Just stand still and take it easy, everything wasn't lost yet. He sweated as he gripped the pliers tighter in his fingers. What would happen now? It had not occurred to him that someone might disturb them right at the end, had it? His eyes blurred. How they would all laugh at him for having started something and then messed it up like this! And Schierl was sure to take him to task, and then they would probably lock him up, or chuck him out of Q. The action he had dreamed about was lost somewhere in the darkness which enveloped him and all that remained was derision and nothingness. So that was it – he was no good at anything. People would not talk about him and his deeds. His knees felt weak. In front of himself he saw a dark, gaping abyss. So that was how it would end. And it had started so well. Tomorrow already the boys might have been whispering about it, about what Charlie had done. He had almost managed to become one of them. He would have thrown each of them a piece of the margarine, nonchalantly, as though it were the most natural thing in the world for him to have it and to give it away. Well, he wouldn't do that now; he would do nothing. They'd all think him a bloody fool, that was all.

Suddenly he spoke up: 'Beat it! I'll cover you.'

His voice was hoarse now. He took a short step to get in front of Tony Fetman and Oscar Kleiner, who was rubbing his behind against the wall. The pliers in his right hand, he was ready to strike. He was going on up to the summit of the only deed life had allotted him so far.

Yes, he told himself, on the verge of tears. He had to do it.

The dark figure was only a little distance away now.

Charlie locked his teeth, shaking all over, and raised the hand holding the pliers.

'Charlie!' whispered Oscar Kleiner. 'Not this! Don't!'

Tony was frightened by the thought of something he had never experienced before. He felt as if he were standing on the brink of a deep, stone well and at the same time as if tongues of flame were licking at him. Whatever happened, perhaps they'd still get away. He'd do it himself if necessary, he was no funk, but not this!

The lamp approached.

It was a woman with a child on her arm. Charlie could not see her as yet, hidden as she was in the shadows. He was standing by himself in the bend of the passage below the staircase. Now for the last step, and then he'd strike.

The child whimpered suddenly. They were right in front of him.

Charlie closed his eyes, sprang, and hit out.

'Let's go!' he said hoarsely.

The woman leaned against the wall, swayed but did not fall. The pliers fell to the ground, ringing with a curious sound that seemed to roll about, long and clear, in the passage like a bronze bell.

The tongues of flame in front of Tony Fetman's eyes disappeared.

'Come here, you idiots!' he said. 'Let's take it with us.'

Oscar was holding his trousers up and Charlie was staring unseeingly ahead of him.

'That woman will come to in a minute, so hurry up!' Tony Fetman urged them in a sibilant whisper. 'Why, she's staring at us already!'

Charlie still had his eyes fixed on nothing.

'Don't stand there gaping and come along!' Tony ordered him.

The child was crying.

Tony Fetman caught both of them by the shoulder.

'This way!'

Dragging the sack behind them, they crept out of the passage and along the low wall outside. The policeman was still dozing under his little roof at the end of the street and the rain was soaking his cap.

Not daring to stop, they hurried through the streets, the cobbles under their feet glistening with rain.

Charlie was terrified by the slightest sound. What's happened to that woman? he wondered. He had socked her good and hard, that was a fact.

Silent streets, and then, at last, Room 16.

The room welcomed them fast asleep, unaware of what had taken place. Nobody was awake.

They hid the sack in Charlie's bunk.

'Nobody will suspect *you* . . .' said Tony.

He did not even protest. He felt as if he were drunk.

Immensely tired, he lay down fully dressed next to the sack. As he stared dully at the wall he saw in front of him the white face of the woman and heard the child weeping and the sound of the falling pliers ringing and ringing, and all of a sudden Charlie cried out.

'Shut up!' hissed Oscar Kleiner.

Tony Fetman crept up to his bunk. 'Be quiet, Charlie,' he said. 'D'you want to give the game away now we're back?'

Charlie moaned intermittently.

'Don't worry,' whispered Tony. 'The woman was standing up, you only rapped her on the nut, that's all. And people must have come right away, only they wouldn't know what it was all about. So you've nothing to be afraid of, you mutt, she's alive, sure she's alive . . . you understand . . .'

But at the same time as he was trying to convince Charlie, he was also trying to figure out how to get rid of the sack first thing in the morning.

'. . . so don't be a bloody fool; and go to sleep,' he concluded, then climbed down and returned to his bunk.

But Charlie kept on sighing. He could hear the heavy breathing of Tony Fetman and Oscar Kleiner. How come they can sleep? he thought enviously. On the other hand, he was not sure that they were both really asleep. More probably not. He himself was suffocating under the weight of the ceiling, which seemed to hang so close above him, threatening to fall and squash him on his bunk. So that was to have been it: his ticket of admission to Room 16, the boat in which he was to sail out on to the surface of their recognition, something intoxicating and enthralling, the legend of a deed, a nice little legend to warm the heart, even laced with a touch of envy as the boys would repeat it before going to sleep. A terrible disappointment nailed him to the bunk. Thus he lay until morning, conscious of nothing but this bottomless disenchantment, everything inside him stifled and numb. He wished fervently for the light of day, yet when at last it came, the darkness of the night seemed more merciful to him.

The morning found him horribly pale, with large blue rings under his eyes. He got up feeling very unsure of himself, disappointment inside him and all over him.

Oscar Kleiner lay with his back turned to Tony Fetman. He, too, was not far from fainting.

No, Oscar Kleiner was not a real hunter like Tony Fetman, after all. He was better at selling things.

Tony was the most cheerful of the three.

'Nothing's happened, you chumps!' he said to them by way of encouragement.

And then, as they were all three standing side by side in the washroom, drying themselves with Oscar's towel:] 'You'd better sell the stuff straightaway today, Oscar. And wipe your glasses!'

Oscar looked around apprehensively, afraid that someone might overhear.

'What?' he asked, adding desperately: 'But where?'

'Well, what d'you think? Of course it's all up to you, pal,' Fetman said, looking derisively at both of them, from Charlie to Oscar, and from Oscar to Charlie.

Oscar nodded sadly. 'All right, I'll try . . .'

'You can keep my share,' said Charlie in a faint voice.

'Don't talk daft,' said Tony.

'You'd get nothing out of it . . .'

'No, really, I don't want anything,' Charlie repeated.

It wasn't that he was afraid, he told himself. If they were found out it would be too late even if he didn't get anything out of it.

Then he went to have another wash. The cold water made him feel better. I am not going to get anything out of it, he thought, and he felt as if a weight had been lifted from him, repeating it over and over to himself as he had said it aloud a while ago. The feeling that had crushed him all night long, the apprehension that he would, in the light of day, be disgusted with himself, that he would be afraid to go out into the street, that dreadful feeling had passed. He would have to look frequently at that house, he told himself. Perhaps the woman really *was* alive.

In the yard he collected a pickaxe and a spade, and in the same leisurely way as always – only his face showing a noticeable pallor – he quietly and without rancour greeted Schierl and walked off towards the town hall, to the building site on the left of the ghetto.

Stephen and Anne

H E lay there quietly.

The beam he was gazing up at had a dark, nut-brown colour. On it somebody had scribbled the word *quarantine*. It struck him as funny that the walls here inside should be the same red colour as the outside walls. He already had his bed – a narrow strip of the paving-stone floor. In the semi-darkness he could make out the rounded shapes of the women, who were getting ready to lie down in the uncertain, flickering light of the candles. He had been lying here in this way for many seconds, in the grip of a fever he was not even aware of, and full of tantalizing thoughts.

Then he fell asleep. He would come awake, wild with desperation, thinking that it was almost dawn, would close his eyes again, desiring to protract the delicious darkness in which he dropped, rose and dropped anew.

He awoke early in the morning.

Astonished, he looked around to find out where he was.

Next to him slept a girl, covered by knapsacks and a dark blanket, on his other side an old man who snored with the exertion of sleep.

He narrowed his eyes and saw her clearly like the white summit of some snow-capped mountain. Her brow was smooth and her skin well-nigh transparent, she had loosely flowing golden hair, and an equally fair nape. The violence with which her image kept returning to him frightened him.

He waited for her to wake. Her hair was like autumn leaves, her lips were pale and half-open. He felt a current pass through him, a current in which there was the light of dawn and the quiet of night.

She sat up, slightly startled.

140

She covered her face with her long fingers.

'Good morning,' he said.

'Good morning.'

'Please don't be angry that I am lying here,' he said. 'I didn't see properly last night.'

'It doesn't matter,' she replied.

She looked across him to where the old man was lying.

'Are you getting up?' he asked.

'Yes, I am,' she said.

'Have you been here long?'

'A week,' she replied.

And then: 'I was already asleep when you arrived.'

'We came in the night,' he said.

'Some transports do come at night,' she replied.

'We don't even know each other,' he said.

She smiled, and he could see both bitterness and embarrassment on her lips.

'My name is Stephen,' he said.

'Mine is Anne,' she replied. And she repeated it: 'Anne.'

An official appeared on the threshold of the wooden staircase.

'It's one of ours,' she said. 'He has got a star.'

A wave of silence swamped the attic.

'What's he want?'

'He is going to read out the names,' she said.

'Our names?'

'Yes, perhaps our names, too,' she replied.

The official stopped a few paces away from them. He spread out his papers like huge bank-notes. Then he said that those whom he was going to read out had been selected by the Council of Elders – entrusted with this task by the German H.Q. – and would go and live in the ghetto.

'And the others?'

'Elsewhere,' she said.

'Where?'

'Nobody knows,' she replied.

And then: 'In the East,' she said.

The old man next to them was awake now. He was holding a wrinkled, sallow hand to his ear, so as to hear better. 'My name is Adam,' he said. 'Adam,' he mumbled.

'Haven't you been read yet?' Stephen asked her.

'No,' she said.

Suddenly she felt ashamed that they had not read her yet.

'My name is Adam,' murmured the old man.

Then Stephen's name was read out.

'That's you,' she said. 'Stephen.'

'Perhaps he'll read you, too,' he said.

He did not.

'Be glad,' she said.

He was silent, frightened suddenly by the infinitude of leave-taking that clung to him.

'Don't cry,' he said.

'I'm not crying,' she replied.

The official announced that those whose names had been called were to go downstairs into the courtyard within ten minutes.

'Just those I've read out – neither more nor fewer,' he said curtly.

Then he added: 'I've not thought this up – it's orders from H.Q.'

'Adam,' the old man repeated.

The official left.

'Are you thinking about it?'

'No,' she answered.

'They'll read you tomorrow,' he said. 'Or some other time.'

He could not make himself stand up, yet he knew he would have to.

He took her hand.

'Come and see me, won't you?' she said.

'I'll come,' he replied.

'We have known each other so short a time,' she said.

'I'll come for sure,' he said again. 'I'm alone here. We can be friends.'

'If they leave us here,' she said.

'Why?'

'I've heard things.'

'What things?'

'That we are to be sent on,' she said. 'Maybe within a week.'

He helped her with the knapsacks.

'You're lucky,' she said.

He was looking at her, unable to reply.

The current rose up in him from somewhere deep inside, right to the top and back again to his finger tips with which he was touching the palm of her hand.

'Perhaps,' she said quietly, 'I shall still be here.'

'You will,' he muttered.

And then he added: 'Certainly you will.'

'Go on, then,' she said.

He looked at her, and he again felt the current, being drowned in it. Then he got up, letting her hand slip out of his, and something stopped inside him; he felt it in the contraction of his chest and the smarting of his eyes that increased with each step he drew farther away from her.

'Adam,' mumbled the old man.

Then he ran along L Avenue; everything that had enveloped him like a spider's web and that alternately burned and went out inside him, alternately driving him forward and drawing him back to the attic of the *quarantine,* turned over inside him and reverberated like the echo of those words.

He put down his knapsack on the bed assigned to him.

Then he ran back the way he had come, not caring what would become of him and his things.

He dashed inside. He saw her, so slim, on the grey palliasse.

'Stephen,' she said.

Then: 'It's you.'

And finally: 'So you've come.' She lowered her eyes.

'Annie,' he said.

'I didn't really expect . . .' she said.

He ignored the old man, whose snoring disturbed all who were near him. He sat down at her side on the mattress, out of which the straw projected like so many arrows. He did not feel any need to say more than that one word he had said already.

'Annie,' he repeated.

He embraced her shoulders and felt the current surging up from inside. The feeling that he was protecting her with the hand that touched her stifled him.

He sat silently next to her, in front of the barrier of stone that was the old man, whose glassy eyes did not take them in and whose sallow neck, resembling a human tree trunk, shielded them from view.

Suddenly his eyes met those of the old man.

'What is it?' she asked.

'Nothing,' he replied.

He could feel that she was afraid. She pressed herself closer to him.

Then she saw the old man's gaze and she was frightened by what she read in it – a wild, imploring insolence and an inquisitive envy.

'My name is Adam,' the old man muttered.

He kept holding his hand up to his face to catch the sound of words that did not reach him.

'Let's get away from here,' said Stephen.

'Yes, let's,' she said.

Then she added: 'What if the official comes?'

'Why should he?'

Her eyes fell and she looked at the floor.

'Let's go, then,' she said.

She did not dare to look again into the dark pools of the old man's eyes. She rose. She had on a coat of some warm, blue material.

Looking at her, the coat and everything else seemed to him to be as clear and clean as the sky.

He had to step across the old man's mattress.

He knew he would speak to him.

'Look after Anne's things,' he said.

And to Anne it seemed as if only these words really woke the old man. He dropped the hand that had acted as a hearing aid. His almond-brown eyes grew wide and soft.

'Adam,' he said.

Then he added: 'Right oh! You run along, children!'

She had to lower her eyes once more.

'Is that your brother?' the old man asked.

They looked at each other. He felt the current again running through him.

'Yes,' he replied for her.

They went out, and it seemed to them that everything they looked at was without a shadow.

And Stephen wished that the current should pass through the tips of his fingers to Anne, that she might feel in that touch the sun, and hope, and the rosy rays of day and its light.

'Brother and sister,' he said.

And then: 'More than that.'

They walked round the blacksmith's shop. On the other side of the slope that towered above the town they saw the rambling building of the Council of Elders.

'If only I had an uncle here,' she said.

'Has he gone?' he asked.

She turned her face to his and, with her finger quite close to him, tapped her forehead.

'Silly,' she said, 'I was thinking of an uncle who does not exist.'

'Are you alone?'

'Completely,' she replied.

'Are you hungry?'

'What could you do about it?'

'Do you know where I live?'

'No,' she said.

'Here,' he said. 'Wait a second.'

He ran upstairs and pulled a piece of cake out of his knapsack; this he broke in two, leaving one of the halves to the ɔoys who were watching him.

'For your hunger,' he said when he was downstairs again.

'Thanks,' she said.

Suddenly they both laughed.

'Let's go back there,' she said then.

J

'There?' he asked.

'Yes,' she said.

'Yes,' he repeated.

When they were sitting down again, he said: 'They'll read you tomorrow.'

'Oh, I'm not thinking about it,' she said.

'There are other things apart from that,' he said.

'What things?'

'Other things,' he repeated.

Then they went out, but they only had time to walk once round the town.

The darkened trees began to merge with their own shadows, the twilight toying with the leaves.

'Come,' she said. 'I'll accompany you.'

He gazed into her eyes, so close to his. He put his arm around her shoulders, which were frail and gentle, making him think it was up to him to protect her. The strong feeling that seemed to have a life of its own inside him and rose in waves up to his throat and farther, both the light and the dark curve of her silhouette, that which at once constricted him and released him from the shadows, holding out the promise of a sensation of freedom, all this flowed into the single word which he now uttered:

'Anne!'

'Stephen!'

He kissed her on the mouth.

'I've never . . . been like this before,' she said.

It was his first kiss as well as hers.

And he again felt those waves returning, clean and fragrant, and he kissed her lips and eyes, which were now filled with tears, and felt a desperate longing that he need never, even at the price of death, live otherwise than at this moment.

They walked a little way from the door, to the spot where a yellow, wooden fence divided off the ghetto from the H.Q.

They shivered with the chill of evening.

'It's not so late yet,' she said.

'Annie,' he said.

'Where shall we go?' she asked.

'Annie,' he repeated.

'We'll have to be going,' she said, and stood still. He felt the irrevocability of the hour that closes the day like a thin sword-blade having the power to cut even the invisible current some-where deep inside where no one can see.

He led her wordlessly round the block of houses next to Q 710. He was aware that some outside influence was disturb-ing that current inside him, and yet he was glad he was walk-ing by her side and feeling her warmth, and at the same time unhappy because he knew what was coming; his throat was constricted by the same huge hoop that was encircling his chest and pressing against his eyes.

'Annie,' he said.

'Yes?' she replied.

And then, after a long silence: 'If you want, Stephen,' she said, 'come and see me in the night.'

'I will,' he whispered. He felt as though she had cut through ropes which had until now bound him.

'Yes, I will,' he said again. 'I'll come for sure.'

'You can go across the courtyards,' she said.

Then she added: 'That's how they do it here.'

'Yes,' he said.

'We'll be moved soon,' she said. 'I feel it.'

'I'll come,' he repeated.

'I feel it somehow,' she said.

And then, 'I'm terribly afraid. It's even worse now.'

'Don't worry,' he said. 'I'll come for sure.'

'It's not far across the courtyards,' she said.

'Yes,' he said.

He took off his coat and threw it over her.

She returned it to him.

Then, all at once, she ran off, suddenly and unexpectedly. She tore herself away from his hands, regretting that she had said what she did. She knew the laws of the ghetto a week longer than he. He only heard her steps, receding into the darkness.

A fraction of that moment was before his eyes every second that passed by, deepening the darkness, these fractional parts of the picture composing a huge mosaic which contained the current and her half-open lips and her tears.

Then the boys became quiet and went to sleep.

He knew he would stay awake. He pieced together the fragments of the night, and only when it seemed to him that the stillness was going to overwhelm him with its immense, unbearable weight, did he steal from his bed.

He jumped over the knapsacks and shoes lying in the middle of the room, and stood by the door. He reached out for the handle. In the instant in which the cool contact poured a whole ocean into his brain, the shining brass growing dull under the imperceptible shadow of his palm, he was again conscious of the warm waves and heard the creaking of the wooden stairs that led up to the attic. At that moment he heard his heart beating, a bronze bell tolling inside him. He pressed down the handle, cautiously but firmly.

The ocean poured itself out into emptiness.

The room was locked.

He felt the soft blow. The earth fell away beneath him. He swallowed his tears. Now he could see the emptiness, and in it a small face and the transparent skin of her forehead, that indescribably fragile something that filled him with a feeling that there was a reason for his existence, those frightened eyes and that breath bitter like almonds.

He crept back to his bed, and then again to the door.

The white square, full of an overpowering silence, gave back a mute echo of the brotherhood he felt for her, a brotherhood that from that moment elevated him above this world and at the time flung him down to its very bottom.

He rattled the handle.

'Be quiet!' someone shouted.

And added something else.

He tried to make himself believe that she could see him all the way from where she was, through the silken web of the night, that it was all one great window, and that behind it was she.

Then he lay on his back, his eyes fixed on the grey ceiling, upon which was her image, indistinct and hazy, but clear in all its details – her eyes and lips. Her hair fell loosely down in the shadows and her voice sounded in the stillness.

His eyes smarted. He was aware of this only every now and again, in the intervals of his imaginings in which he heard every word a thousand times and once, as a single word, and then as one great silence.

She penetrated everything: the white door and the stillness of the night.

She returned to him in his feverish visions, and he walked with her, his hand on her shoulder, and the waves rose and fell in him and filled both of them.

In the morning he ran, breathless, through the town.

He flew upstairs.

All he found was an empty attic.

The transport to the East had left in the night.

Blue Flames

THE taller of the two gendarmes frowned and repeatedly cleared his throat; he had had an uneasy feeling right from the moment when he first entered the ghetto. The two of them were just passing the bandstand of the Ghettoswingers, and the shrilling of the trumpets did not abate in the slightest. The gendarme's weary mind vaguely registered the shouts of the brown-tanned youths, calling someone named Woodpecker and exhorting him not to slack, but sing; he replied by saying they could all go to hell because he was on his way to the blacksmith's shop to get some exercise. Then they waggled their shoulders and yelled:

> Up and down and down and up
> Our ship goes rolling.

The gendarme was irritated, and felt a desire to hit the boy. It was a persistent feeling, and he could not get rid of it.

'They're crazy!' he said, bending down slightly towards his smaller companion. 'In this heat.'

'They're on a ship,' grinned the other. 'It's not so hot there.'

He pushed his helmet a little to the back of his head and blew beads of perspiration off his lips.

The taller gendarme had pale, cheese-coloured cheeks in a lean, pock-marked face. The collar of his service blouse stood out stiffly from his emaciated neck. As he tried to moisten his dry lips, his Adam's apple jogged up and down in his throat.

'Still,' he repeated, 'in this heat!'

'What do you care – here?' said the smaller one.

The taller one did not reply any more. Now and again he nodded his long, horse-like head, sleepily, without moving his

150

parched lips. His distrustful, green eyes scanned everyone in
the street, but he said nothing and never stopped. They tra-
versed the town with long, quick strides, like a knife cutting
bread.

'They say Holler is behind it all,' the smaller one spoke up
after a while.

'That's what I say,' said the taller one wearily. To himself
he swore at the heat.

'It stands to reason,' he added, 'that if you make such a
racket, you'll only get more knocked about.'

'More or less,' replied the smaller one. 'If you were here
you wouldn't care.'

The dusty smell of the chestnuts and lime trees clung to
their mouths.

'Phew!' spat the tall one.

'If the commandant has allowed them to, why shouldn't
they have a little fun?' muttered the smaller one with a frown.

'Even so,' the taller one insisted.

Their heavy army issue boots slid along the paving, and they
listened to the clinking of their hobnails. That was an ordinary
pleasant sound, but above and beneath it squawked the jazz.
The youths behind their backs roared as if they were drunk.

'What's that coming?' asked the taller one suddenly, and
licked his lips.

Before the other could reply, a carriage came into view and
rattled towards them.

The taller one slowed his pace a little.

A piebald horse with white and grey spots scattered over his
rump jutted out of the silver-polished harness. Enthroned in
the purple of the now much-faded blankets which covered up
the patches in the upholstery of the seat behind the coachman,
sat Ignatz Marmulstaub, member of the Council of Elders.

'Will he stop?' asked the taller gendarme inquiringly.

'He might,' replied the other.

'He should,' the tall one corrected him. In spite of all the
compassion he felt for this town because it was a Czech town,
he felt pleased that here at last was something he could tackle;

a job worthy of a sergeant of the gendarmerie who was already half on duty; and on the other hand the responsibility of someone who would never be freed from the obligation of accounting for himself to the gendarmes on the highway.

'Mr Marmulstaub,' the coachman said in a confidential undertone as he half turned towards him, 'the gendarmes!'

'Where?' came from his passenger. 'Ah! In front of us. You'll have to go slower.'

He leaned out of the coach.

'Your obedient servant, gentlemen,' he said in a gruff voice. And he was going to add something about the weather and the heat.

They did not as much as raise their eyes.

'Do you think he ought to stop?' the taller one asked his companion, bending down towards him.

'He could,' said the smaller one.

'Rightly speaking, he should,' the taller gendarme insisted in a loud and stubborn voice.

Marmulstaub coloured, thinking: too late to stop now. He had simply missed it. And then: they weren't addressing him. On the contrary: they didn't even respond to his greeting. And anyway, they didn't call him back, and they looked so uncouth in their polished helmets covered with green cloth.

'He drives about like a bloody king,' murmured the taller gendarme angrily without moving his narrow head.

'Well, that's not such a big impertinence,' replied the smaller one, 'considering the heat.'

'Bloody cheek, I call it,' countered the taller one.

'They drew to the side,' said the smaller one in a languid tone. 'That's enough for me.'

'They couldn't do less,' added the tall one.

'We were in the middle of the road, and our boots are for pedestrians,' the smaller one replied calmly.

'Too much molly-coddling, that's what I say,' complained the taller one.

'Oh, well, it's so terribly hot, chum,' the smaller one evaded a reply. He had actually meant to say it wasn't worth talking

about. Now he took his helmet off. He had sparse, straw-
coloured hair, wet and crumpled with perspiration.

'It is that,' agreed the taller one, and he too lapsed into
silence.

Then he swallowed some saliva he had laboriously gathered
on his tongue. The Adam's apple, which protruded like a
knuckle of a fist rammed inside his throat, leaped erratically
upwards and fell again.

They passed through a narrow gate in the fence which ran
round the ghetto. The concert in the main square was only a
barely perceptible sound now, almost inaudible. The SS man
who walked up and down the other side of the fence was given
a perfunctory salute and replied in the same mute way.

The smaller gendarme put on his helmet.

2

'No,' Marmulstaub answered the coachman when they had
reached the square. 'Don't wait for me.'

He had decided not to use the carriage any more. It attracted too much attention to himself, as he could see from his
encounter with the gendarmes. And others, too, were irritated
by it, he could see that right now by looking at the people in
the square.

'You know what?' he said. 'Take the carriage away for
repairs. It creaks abominably.'

'It creaks all right,' replied the coachman, who was just
thinking the same thing, 'because I have nothing to grease it
with.'

Just as he left, the music stopped.

'What's up?' someone asked Marmulstaub.

'Why?' he replied. 'I don't know.'

'Can't you hear it?'

'What should I hear?' he asked, but at that very moment he,
like everyone else, heard the murmur of the car belonging to
Herr von Holler, which carried through the cleft of sudden

silence, the car's klaxon cutting across the hush of the crowd and ringing out sharply over their heads. Ignatz Marmulstaub, however, was quick to notice that Herr von Holler, the ghetto commandant, was not in the car, its only occupant a mere private of the Signals Corps.

The crowd thinned out.

'Why don't you go on playing,' he said in a hoarse voice. This wretched town, he thought, hangs its tail and sits on its backside even when it doesn't have to. After all, he had turned his back on these gendarmes a while ago, and nothing happened.

He delighted in their almost tangible astonishment. The people kept their eyes glued to his face as though they could interpret even the motions of his lips and tried to guess in advance what shape his thoughts would take.

'You can go on playing!' he repeated huskily.

He noted with pleasure that the concert was beginning anew. At that moment he caught sight of little Liselotte.

She, too, had seen and heard him, was his first thought. In the joy that welled up in him he forgot all about the gendarmes.

'Good afternoon, miss,' he greeted her, narrowing his eyes.

'Good day,' she replied.

'It's a fine day today, and there's music,' he said. 'Quite a change, isn't it.'

'But it's also advisable to keep out of sight because one can't tell what might happen. That is another change.'

'What could happen?' he smiled. 'After all, everything has already happened.'

'I have more errands than I have leisure in any case,' she said. 'Even though there is music.'

'Can I help you in any way?' he inquired.

'No, it's all women's stuff,' he said.

'Still, I might be able to do something for you,' he suggested.

'I must do it myself,' she said quickly, noticing at the same time how he was looking her all over.

'Always without me, Miss Liselotte,' he said reproachfully.
'Always without me.'

'Good-bye!'

'Yes,' he muttered, more to himself than to her.

He threw his jacket over his other arm. With his right hand
he now began, swiftly and impatiently, to wipe his perspiring
brow, and to scratch himself on the chest and under the arm-
pits. His face went red, for he felt that the little one had lied
to him. He had accurate information about her, let her not
forget that, and he knew what he knew.

He stood there jacketless, with large, round shoulders, and
with his head bowed heavily over his chest, his shirt unbuttoned right down to the semi-circle of the trousers top. From
under drawn brows he followed what went on around him,
watching the chap with a conductor's baton as he carved tri-
angles in the hot air.

Then his eyes began to rove, appraising the clusters of
human bodies. Here and there his gaze would rest, and he
would narrow his large, dark eyes, which then took on a deep
purplish tinge as they merged with the reddish swollen pouches
under his eyes and the red-coloured mesh of thread-like veins
in the corners.

The sun was burning hot, and the women were dressed in
the lightest of frocks. His eyes travelled hungrily along the
white thighs of girls, slipping right down, down their calves to
the ankles and back again, up along their throats now shining
with beads of perspiration, and their red or pale lips. In each
and every one of them he saw, in his mind's eye, something of
Liselotte, her narrow waist and her breasts resembling small,
halved apples. Eagerly he linked his imaginings with the sound
of her voice and with her scent. Hot blood pulsed through his
veins. Yet, despite this internal fire, his appearance was one of
almost immovable tranquillity, the only sign of life, indeed,
being the constant rubbing together of his extraordinarily
small, delicate and white hands.

A little way from the railing stood small, thirteen-year-old
girls from L 410. He felt them all over with his purplish gaze

out of narrowed eyes, saying to himself that here there were no
little girls.

But he was disturbed by the glances he knew were being
directed at his back.

3

For some time now Herr von Holler had been looking out
for his car, which was not back yet. Then he left the window,
walked slowly across the room, and reached for the telephone,
studying the pinkish crescents on his finger-nails and listening
to the gentle whirring of the fan.

He dialled a number and waited.

'Von Holler,' he said at last. 'Heil Hitler! Why am I calling
you? Do you want to be present this evening at Löwenbach's
interrogation?'

In his mind's eye he saw the small courier in civilian clothes.

'Heil Hitler!' said a voice. 'When?'

'Tonight, if you have no other programme.'

'Not really,' rasped the voice.

'It'll be good fun,' the commandant continued, trying to
prolong the conversation. 'The fat one is going to assist. The
one you saw yesterday. I've just sent for him.'

'I remember,' said the voice. 'You have an inexhaustible
sense of humour.'

'You flatter me,' said Herr von Holler. 'But sometimes it is
necessary. Just imagine you were cleaning the dung-heap and
then took a hot bath.'

'One day you're going to lose that Jew of yours,' crackled
the voice at the other end. 'I hope you will not miss him.'

'His time hasn't come yet,' said the commandant.

'Not willing?' hooted the voice.

'For the time being,' parried Herr von Holler.

'Exaggerated,' came from the receiver.

'Someone has to be the last. That's no advantage. Let it be
him.'

'You cannot do without one ugly Jew, but on the other hand you want us to bleed the ghetto and rid you of a whole half of them at a time.'

'You must understand, he's my secret weapon. Apart from the knout, the bullet, and the rope. Often a single word is enough. A word from him, that is.'

'In short, that rotten Jew of yours is so excellent,' clanged the voice, 'that he is on velvet and doesn't even know it.'

'I wouldn't like to enlarge upon it over the telephone,' evaded the commandant.

'One of these days we'll put him in the waxworks for you,' chuckled the voice. 'You and your pet Jew!'

Herr von Holler did not reply for a moment. Did that half-grown civilian nincompoop think, he said to himself, that just because he was a courier plying between Berlin and the H.Q. he could threaten him? Of course his, von Holler's, fortress was over-populated. That wouldn't matter so much for its own sake, he thought, but it did matter in view of the forthcoming filming of the ghetto!

'Well then, if you want to come,' von Holler said in a tone which indicated that the conversation was at an end, 'I'll give you a call.'

'Accepted with thanks,' came the voice. 'What time?'

'At eight.'

'Right!' replied the voice.

And the phone went dead.

Von Holler began to pace the room with long strides, tall and bony, proud of his noble origin and of his ability to put on a rough or genteel air, according to who his interlocutor was. If only he knew the extent and the limits of the authority vested in the man from Berlin, he would find the right tone for dealing with him, too.

He stopped by the table. Picking up some papers, he glanced through the lists of names which Marmulstaub had brought him, scanning them with curious eyes. But the weak glimmer of interest quickly vanished – they were names for a museum. They lacked the romantic touch which they had once possessed. Then his gaze was attracted by the dark brown desk diary with the von Holler coat of arms. Thursday had been ticked off for some reason. Oh yes, he recalled, today Marmulstaub's jazz band was performing. And the fat one would most likely be there. What a pity he had not thought of telling the officer who had gone to fetch Marmulstaub.

4

Meanwhile the coachman had unharnessed the piebald outside the town gate between two slopes.

'The Council of Elders has sent me,' he said. 'Namely Mr Marmulstaub. The carriage needs a complete overhaul. It was idle for a long time.'

'Mr Marmulstaub is going to drive in it?' asked the blacksmith, doubtfully inspecting the gig.

'All the gentlemen from the Council are going to drive in it,' the coachman rebuffed him.

From the blacksmith's shop came the monotonous clatter of hammers.

'Hallo, boy!' the blacksmith, a lean man with clever eyes called into the open door. 'Come here a moment.'

A lanky youth in a leather apron came out.

'This is Woodpecker,' said the blacksmith. 'We'll give him the job.'

'Overjoyed,' said the youth. 'What's this for? A coronation?'

'Something like that. It's for the greater glory of the town,' said the lean one.

'Delighted,' muttered the boy angrily.

'Don't make fun of it,' the coachman murmured, turning to the blacksmith. 'That's neither nice nor proper.'

'This is overtime work, isn't it?' complained Woodpecker. 'And for what? Three kicks for lunch! And there is music in the square.'

'Mr Woodpecker,' the coachman said to the boy, 'we need it soon.'

Then he itemized all the faults of the vehicle.

'All right, then. Tomorrow,' said the blacksmith. 'Suit you?'

'Suits me fine,' said the coachman.

He patted the horse on the muzzle, and was annoyed to see Woodpecker offer it an empty palm, which the piebald licked rewardlessly. He walked away with the horse-collar and harness over his left arm. He was an elderly man, and his burden made him bend almost double.

The boy made no move to help him. As soon as he was alone with the gig, he aimed a vicious kick at it. It was considerably dilapidated. He scratched the backs of his hands, and lost even the last vestige of inclination to start the work of repairing the carriage. The wheels seemed to him to be clocks with plump hands and a transparent face, through which he could see the Ghettoswingers playing in the square, where he had left them not so long ago. Tramp and Mylord among them. And the girls from L 410.

He went off to have a wash.

'I'm going,' he told the blacksmith, who was a bachelor and lived over the shop. 'I know pretty well what's wrong with it now, and I've repaired a thing or two already.'

'That'll do,' said the blacksmith. 'It's too hot today, anyway, and you still have a restless nature. You can finish it tomorrow, so that the frog shan't croak.'

5

The German automobile was coming back. Herr von Holler's dispatch rider had taken to the Council of Elders the food ration papers which were normally delivered by the Council's chairman, Löwenbach. It was actually for these papers that he went to the H.Q. shortly after lunch, and he had not come back. The sound of the klaxon, its clamour shattering the curtain of silence, was again borne above the crowd.

The eyes of the crowd sought comfort in the face of Ignatz Marmulstaub. Again as before, he felt he was the centre of

their attention, and he was again pleased by it. Somewhere in
that crowd, he told himself, was little Liselotte. The thought
that she, too, witnessed how he was looked up to took away
the bitterness of the thoughts that preceded it.

Then he actually saw her.

Some tall youth behind him was shouting, with a whole
gang of boys accompanying him:

> Wiggle your backside,
> You lazy girl!

He saw at once that it was meant for her, and he wondered
that she only smiled inanely and pretended not to hear.

One of the youths began to spit, aiming at the toes of Marmulstaub's shoes.

'Good shot, Tramp!' the others yelled.

Irritated, Marmulstaub stood aside, stepping on the tall
youth's foot as he did so.

'Sorry,' he murmured.

'Like hell,' shouted Woodpecker, bending down and nursing
his foot in his hand.

Marmulstaub had turned round and thus lost the little one
from sight.

'Well, wiggle that backside of yours!' hooted Woodpecker
in an angry tone, but more for the benefit of his friends than
of the fat man next to him. 'It's big enough, anyway!'

'Go to the devil,' said Marmulstaub darkly. 'Lout!'

His purplish eyes investigated the crowd. He could not see
her any more.

'After all, I didn't do it on purpose,' he said apologetically.

And suddenly he realized that the looks which the people
were now giving him were not in the least admiring. He was
annoyed by their ill-concealed maliciousness.

'Look at him,' said Woodpecker. 'He swears at me although
he almost crushed my toes. The ugly toad!'

Marmulstaub blenched. Helplessly he stared after Woodpecker, who had easily penetrated the thick throng of people

which had frustrated his efforts at finding the girl. But that did not hurt him any more. That nickname should not have been uttered. He felt sick.

He turned away from the swarming crowd and the syncopated music, accompanied by the wild shouting of the youths who performed all the town's calls and ditties.

He sought to escape from this noisy outer world into the silence of introspection. He no longer perceived the multitude around him and the din – he was quite alone. Now he could ponder the dreadful incompatibility of his own spiritual system and the surrounding world. His was an elevated spirit, the others were rabble. He had the pleasure of something that was infinitely removed from this moment and this town, not only in time or distance.

He did not hear any further derisive echoes. He only felt the cooler air brought here by the wind from the river Oder, and, automatically and without thinking, he put on his jacket. Closing his large, dark violet eyes, he listened to the music that gushed forth on strings of infinite delicacy inside him, a minute web of tones and a wave of images.

6

'Out of the way!' shouted the First Officer as he pushed through the crowd.

He returned to the square. Physical contact with people repelled him. He felt a temptation to pull out his pistol and shoot his way through the throng.

'Make way, you scum!' he yelled. 'Do you hear?'

He had to find that fat pig of a Marmulstaub because the commandant had no one of lesser rank handy, and the dispatch rider had taken the car to deliver those grub papers! And, to crown it all, Marmulstaub was neither at the Council of Elders nor at his home.

'Get away from here!' he yelled. 'All of you!'

K

Then he climbed on to the wooden rail that surrounded the Ghettoswingers.

'Shut up!' he shouted.

And he found that they obeyed him at once, even though he had not even turned round to face them.

'Marmulstaub to me!'

Marmulstaub stood a little farther off. He raised his eyes from the ground and lifted an arm. His small, white palm dangled in the air. He gathered himself together quickly. The darker green uniform, different from that worn by the gendarmes, had frightened him.

The First Officer had already seen him. So he was here, after all, he thought. Satisfied, he climbed down again, motioning the band to resume playing. They did so immediately. You had to yell at the Jews, he told himself. Then they understood.

Marmulstaub's eyes roved the crowd. Was there really only malice in the faces which he passed? Perhaps not, he thought. But he could find no sympathy anywhere. And yet, he told himself, a little while ago they all but kissed his feet, every single one of them.

Herr von Holler's First Officer was waiting for him by the railing, and nobody knew why. Lo, Marmulstaub meditated, there was the Book of Life open in front of him. What would he read in it if it were pushed under his nose? What did the icy reserve which he felt all round him mean?

He stopped at a distance which he felt the officer would consider respectful enough and bent in a deep bow. In his head, which was approaching the dust of the paving, he weighed everything he knew about himself against his estimate of what the others knew, those others who were watching him now. Even thus, with his forehead to the ground which he preferred to look at rather than the uniform (for, in spite of everything, a German uniform still inspired fear in him), even thus he felt his own terrible lack of security.

Yet there was consolation in the knowledge that between the lines of human thought there was always a space in which one could read differently. Marmulstaub slowly straightened himself. Not for a moment did he contemplate revenge against his Jewish town for the hostility he divined behind his back. Did those who did not find his efforts useful want to see his head roll in the dust? Did they wish this through a desire for justice? Or through envy?

He saw his two hands. Well, they were clean, he told himself with satisfaction. Clean. And yet – he thought as he resumed a completely upright posture – and yet they had hung on him an invisible reproach. That nickname . . . And when they feared trouble a while ago, they had bent their gaze on him. And none of them could deny that the well-nigh imperceptible favour shown him by Herr von Holler – so scantily shown at that – was a useful drop in the insignificant ocean of other people's actions.

'If you please,' he said. 'I'm at your service, Herr Commandant Stellvertreter!'

It occurred to him that perhaps he would not even be required to go with the First Officer, in which case the humiliation would be transformed into an honour, for it would mean that this German officer had had to come and find him in order to have a word with him.

'Don't babble!' barked the officer. 'Come on, you're coming with me!'

'May I ask where to, sir?'

'To the commandant's office.'

'On foot?' he inquired politely.

Nevertheless he felt that he could no longer save anything in the eyes of the crowd.

'Naturally on foot, Jew!' said the officer, shaking his head slightly in astonishment and spitting disgustedly.

'Jawohl,' replied Marmulstaub apathetically.

'Stop your chatter and get along!'

But Marmulstaub was not thinking of the reason for this call from the commandant. To that extent at least he was calm. And, as always when anything was about to happen, his mind now fixed again on the vision from which he was forcibly torn only by the external interruption occasioned by the

officer. Carpets in a long, silent corridor. Then he saw a city
within a city, far removed from the hubbub of life, or rather
its present travesty. A citadel of the spirit. A place surrounded
by Rome.

'This way!' shouted the officer.

'At your service, sir,' replied Marmulstaub.

Undisturbed, his imaginings dwelt on in that place. He was
a librarian there, sorting out Judaic documents.

The echoes of distant melodies once again ceased to touch
him. Let the music which he had raised for the town out of the
commandant's very bones and sinews play on without him!
He would remain, as hitherto, but the initiator of everything.
A hawser. A lever. Let others tug and pull, but there had to
be something else, as well; a traction force; a firm point.

He found that at this moment he was quite well disposed
towards that offensive nickname. Almost as though it did not
belong to him.

'Terribly hot today, wasn't it?' he addressed the officer amic-
ably. 'But now it is getting a little cooler at last.'

'Who asked for your opinion, you stinking Jew?' replied the
officer furiously. 'Get a move on! Faster!'

Marmulstaub noted with satisfaction that Herr von Holler's
second-in-command continued to use the formal mode of
address, and he stepped out a trifle quicker.

'I'm coming,' he answered calmly, adding guilelessly:
'Surely we needn't hurry so.'

7

The commandant motioned him to a chair and spoke quite
affably. He had immediately dismissed his deputy, so that they
were alone in the office. He sensed the disquietude of the man
in front of him, and he therefore began the interview more
mildly than he had intended.

'The ghetto, I hear, is indulging in wild music,' he said.

'In moderation, Excellency,' replied Marmulstaub.

'Then that's all right,' said the commandant.

'Certainly, sir,' nodded Marmulstaub. He waited for what was to come. He was sure something was coming, and was prepared to disarm the commandant by prompt acquiescence to everything he might want, in order to avoid any unpleasantness. But the other uniforms he had met earlier that day had weakened him. He knew he was trembling.

'Have you seen Löwenbach?' Herr von Holler asked him.

'No, I haven't,' he replied.

'That's just the point,' said the commandant. 'You should have paid more attention to him.'

Marmulstaub's anxious eyes searched the commandant's sinewy face.

'I don't understand, Excellency,' he quavered.

'Don't be frightened,' added the commandant. 'For the time being he is still alive and well.'

He stopped speaking. Marmulstaub went on trembling.

'I gave him your lists to sign, and he refused. You know that we don't like that sort of thing. Quite apart from the fact that these are to be labour transports and all of them are to come back to us.'

'I am not frightened,' whispered Marmulstaub.

'You will deputize for Löwenbach. That's why I wanted to speak to you.'

'It is too great an honour, sir,' said Marmulstaub, who had grown completely pale.

'Don't be so modest!' said the commandant.

'And Mr Löwenbach?' he asked quickly. 'Has anything happened?'

'I trust he will agree. For the present he is here, downstairs. Let's hope he's not too cold. However, I cannot guarantee it.'

The red colour which had meanwhile again begun to return to Marmulstaub's fat cheeks vanished at once. He had been right in thinking that there were unpleasant things coming. He was now equally sure that this was still not the end of it. The uniform. He had known, hadn't he, that if Herr von Holler were in uniform, it would all be so much the worse. But if

Löwenbach was under arrest, what then? All of a sudden he caught sight of the commandant's narrow slits of eyes and knots of muscle, and he understood: the signature!

'I can't deputize for him,' he whispered. 'The gentlemen of the Council haven't approved the nomination.'

'Don't talk rot! We are not Parliament!'

'I only ventured, Excellency . . .'

'We are going downstairs now to ask Löwenbach if he agrees. I have some business there anyway. I'm only waiting for my guest to arrive.' He glanced at his watch, adding: 'But there's still time.'

'For God's sake, no, Excellency,' murmured Marmulstaub, trembling.

'What are you afraid of?'

'I – I am not afraid, Excellency.'

He saw what was going to happen as clearly as if it were actually taking place before his eyes. The man from Berlin would incite the commandant, and vice versa. In the end, Löwenbach would agree to anything. And he, Marmulstaub, was to be present.

'A transport is being prepared on the basis of these lists, sir,' he began.

'Only preparations are being prepared at present.'

'And Mr Löwenbach's signature . . . Is that so necessary?'

'As far as I am concerned, no,' said the commandant.

'I see,' whispered Marmulstaub, feeling a wild, secret joy at the thought that these tendons and knots of muscle were not omnipotent. There was something that had authority over them.

'And then, it is necessary that things should be done the proper way,' Herr von Holler went on. 'As you know, we have a visitor here. I don't want anything to be missing.'

'And may I ask if there is anything that you miss?' asked Marmulstaub cleverly. All at once he felt calmer.

'Your notes, for instance,' came the crushing reply.

'I took the liberty of supposing, Excellency, that you preferred me to give you my views by word of mouth.'

'How am I to interpret that?' said Herr von Holler. 'As mistrust? Is that what you wish me to read into it?'

'No, sir, no! Please!'

It came to Marmulstaub for the second time that he would have to give in, or the commandant would have him dragged down to the cellar to join Löwenbach. And he saw that this blackmail would continue until he pulled out his fountain-pen. His joy at the unknown authority of his imagination dissolved in the muscular and sinewy face of the commandant.

And yet he decided, in the shadow of the preceding admission of Herr von Holler, to reveal the only thing he knew.

'Excellency, Mr Löwenbach intimated to me that perhaps not all the transports would be labour ones, and that they were not to return.'

'That's why he is in the cellar!' The commandant rose abruptly to his feet.

Marmulstaub felt uneasy sitting down. Still, he said to himself, it worked. His trump card. He got up from his seat too now, feeling sad. After all, when it was by word of mouth he had never refused this fellow anything.

'Yes,' he said quietly.

'That is nothing but swinish propaganda. We punish that here. You know how.'

'Certainly, Excellency. I would myself take measures if it were to spread to the ghetto.'

'That sounds better, Marmulstaub,' muttered Herr von Holler. 'The cellar is big and very cold. It is full of rats. I should hate to see you there too.'

'Thank you,' whispered Marmulstaub.

The commandant sat down again, leaving Marmulstaub to stand.

'Prepare everything for an inspection of the town,' he said. 'I don't want to come across anything that is not in order.'

'In what way, sir?'

'I wish to take my guest round the town. There's going to be trouble if I find anything wrong!'

Marmulstaub, however, was convinced that this was only

the commandant's new ruse to get him to sign. The slight pleasure he had felt at his revelation and at the commandant's having risen from his chair – as well as at the fact that he still had not signed – was gone. At the same time he felt a sharp disappointment at the realization that Herr von Holler was not trembling under the threat that he, Marmulstaub, might tell someone in a position to investigate the matter that the transports were not coming back, while his own body trembled violently at a mere hint from the commandant that he might be put among the rats. With him it was all completely different.

'I had a short list of defects, sir, to which I have for some time been meaning to draw your attention.' And Marmulstaub began to search his pockets.

'But you have it no longer,' said the commandant with chilly, almost indifferent scorn.

'I must have put it somewhere . . .' said Marmulstaub defensively.

After a short pause he added: 'I'll find it by tomorrow.'

If only the commandant did not have his uniform on, he would be easier to talk to.

'That's all,' said Herr von Holler. 'Have you a pen?'

'I have,' Marmulstaub whispered. 'My oral consent, Excellency . . . ?'

'You can keep that!'

The scraping of the nib could be heard distinctly in the silent office.

'Might I go now, Excellency?'

'Don't you want to have a word with Löwenbach?' asked the commandant, and he suddenly felt a strong urge to burst into laughter. If he did take the fat man down, he would surely fall apart, the coward. And then that dwarf from Berlin would think he wasn't fit even for the waxworks.

'I should prefer to go and look for those lists of defects,' said Marmulstaub cautiously.

'Are you afraid of the rats? You fox!'

'No, sir,' replied Marmulstaub. 'Not of the rats.'

'Löwenbach wouldn't bite you,' laughed Herr von Holler. 'All right, you can go.'

The blood came back into the face of the man in the black overcoat so rapidly that the commandant could not keep back an amused smile. But it was not a pleasant smile; it was just as unpleasant as his whole sinewy, muscular and highly coloured face. Better get rid of him, he thought. He was sure to shit himself if he was forced to attend the interrogation. And that, if you please, was his pet Jew, his exhibit! He had secured such a name for him. Had even ensured that he would be the last to go. Perhaps he had really over-rated the fat man's usefulness.

Marmulstaub was filled with an immense relief. But in spite of that relief, from somewhere inside him (where his imaginings created the vision of a pair of hands – someone else's hands and yet somehow also his own – clasped together, fine, white and unsoiled) a feeling of sadness was conveyed to his consciousness, sadness at the fact that he had signed after all. That his signature would remain for all time, and that someone might see how he had helped himself out of trouble. Still, he was happy to see that he enjoyed the commandant's confidence. And happy that he need not be present when Herr von Holler took his guest down to the cellar to Löwenbach. And that he was allowed to leave by himself.

He returned to the town. On the road he met the two gendarmes whom he had already encountered earlier that afternoon.

'Your obedient servant, gentlemen,' he greeted them, and pulled out his pass.

'Well, well,' said the smaller gendarme to the other, 'the gentleman is on foot.'

'And what about the carriage?' jeered the taller one. But he was only speaking to his companion.

They took no notice of his pass.

8

A man from Marmulstaub's office stopped him at the inter-
section of the main L Avenue and the highway.

'Mr Marmulstaub,' he began, 'have you also heard that
there will be new transports?'

'No,' he replied in a friendly voice, 'I haven't heard that.'

He felt a sudden twinge of regret for this town. Tomorrow,
perhaps, it would already begin to shake in its foundations. He
had had to lay before Herr von Holler lists of people which
concerned almost half of the whole town. He decided to be
merciful and to keep back as much as possible. Mustn't tor-
ment them.

'They say that Mr Löwenbach has not returned from the
commandatur,' the man went on. 'He refused to sign something, they say.'

'I know nothing about that,' said Marmulstaub curtly. 'Did
he say anything about it before he left?'

'They say he did,' said the man. 'What do you think – about
the transports?'

'I don't know,' he repeated.

'And Löwenbach – will he come back?'

'I don't know,' he muttered darkly.

'Did they put him in the cellar?'

'Man,' said Marmulstaub, 'are you interrogating me or
what?'

'Someone said,' the clerk continued remorselessly, 'that
they would be labour transports.'

'I tell you I don't know, wretched man, I don't know, really,'
Marmulstaub tried to ward off further questioning. 'If I knew,
I'd tell all of you in time. Everything.'

'And what about our women?' the man rambled on.

'I don't know!'

'Will they come too?'

'Leave me in peace, will you!'

And he walked on, fearing all the time lest he should be bothered again.

The Ghettoswingers were still playing in the square, but only a few people remained to listen. These young greenhorns, Marmulstaub thought, were always carefree. Youths like that one in the afternoon. Nothing ever happened to them. It was because they had no feeling of responsibility, he said to himself. Irresponsible in everything and always. He suddenly felt envy towards the image of Woodpecker, whose face he now pictured in his mind but whom he did not know, and he wished he could, by some process of reincarnation, assume the irresponsibility of that longish, semi-childish face with its expression of impudent innocence, as it remained in his imagination, and could swear at people, calling them frogs and toads. Where could he possibly have put that list of defects which he had thought to remove in co-operation with the commandant's people in the interests of this very town? Could he use this to redeem himself? No, he thought, that was impossible. Löwenbach had thrown the glove too insolently and too far. He would have to pick it up. Then it crossed his mind that it was bad luck that the Kommandant had to think of him, of all people. Still, his hands were clean, because Herr von Holler had to call *somebody*. It might just as easily have been someone else. If it came to anything, he would have to be forgiven. Yes, his hands were clean. He began to pity Löwenbach. He remembered the mention of the rats. Even his thoughts were unsoiled.

He felt tired. Something seemed to weigh him down and choke him. Sad and depressed, he thought of sending for little Liselotte. She had repulsed him in the afternoon, but now, now he could send for her as the deputy of the former chairman Löwenbach.

He entered his house and called a servant.

9

Here they called Liselotte Lizzy. She was sitting in Room 20 of the youth dormitory in Street Q 710.

When Woodpecker had called for her and told her that to-morrow they would be saying good-bye to the Fortress and that they would like to see her before they went, she put on a jacket and came with him.

'I know it already,' she said. 'The sparrows on the roof are chirruping about it.'

'Fine, Lizzy,' he murmured.

'Where are we going? To number 20?'

'That's right, Lizzy,' he said.

'All right then. Let's go,' she replied. She had the feeling that somewhere something was about to end today. She could see no reason why she should refuse. She had refused once before today – in the square that afternoon. The fat fellow, first among those who knew how to make life pleasant for themselves even here and who, she was sure, would always manage to make life pleasant for themselves.

With the agility of a cat she climbed on to one of the top bunks, let her legs swing down, and whistled to herself as she saw the boys' eyes licking her calves. She had been here on several other occasions, but never had there been so many boys.

'Here, some pancakes for you, Lizzy,' said Woodpecker. They ate, washing the food down with water which they all called rum.

'You've used too much garlic,' criticized Lizzy, her mouth full.

'Not us,' said Woodpecker, adding: 'The social worker made them for us.'

'Who's that?' asked Lizzy, and climbed up again.

'Oh, that's a woman,' Woodpecker laughed, 'who gives you a lot of advice, and if you have the squirts, she hides your lunch – in her own stomach. Understand?'

'But she's got to be pretty ugly,' interjected Mylord, 'or she wouldn't take the job.'

'Well, gents,' cut in Tramp, 'tomorrow night hardly half of us will be here. And quite possibly not a single one.'

He jumped up next to Lizzy and put his arm round her shoulders.

She looked at him in surprise and threw away a toothpick she had in her hand.

But then she understood without having to ask.

'Hey, Tramp,' called Mylord, the Ghettoswingers' first trumpet-player, 'give Lizzy our best wishes.'

Then they started to talk in whispers.

Tramp pulled the blanket so that it hung down curtain-wise across his bunk.

'Throw us up that rum!' he demanded.

Woodpecker threw him a bottle of water. All they saw was Tramp's hairy hand as it stretched out, caught the bottle, and vanished.

The Kid sat by himself a little apart from the others.

Having earlier distributed the contents of a parcel he had received from his parents, he was now reading a letter admonishing him to look after himself and to come home in good health.

Tramp jumped down.

Lizzy was drinking; they could all hear the water gulping in her throat.

When Mylord climbed down she began to sing.

'Not bad,' commented Mylord. 'Woodpecker's turn.'

Woodpecker heard how they all accompanied Lizzy's singing, and he continued to hum to himself even when the others had stopped.

> I'll get me a new pair of skates
> or behind a nunnery's gates
> unburden my heavy heart.

Then all was just that song.

'How about an interval?'

Woodpecker was back with the others.

'Don't be silly,' called out Lizzy. 'Later.'

Woodpecker was fastening his trousers with a piece of string. The song kept sounding in his ears. There was everything in it. Something that was behind him and something a long way ahead. And also this moment. He tied a knot on the string.

One by one the boys climbed up and, after a while, clambered down again.

The Tramp bowed in front of the Kid.

'For God's sake, how many more?' said Lizzy in a thick voice.

'She's a bitch,' said Woodpecker under his breath, 'but she has staying power.'

'Christ's sake, Lizzy,' pleaded Mylord. 'You wouldn't let the Kid go away immaculate, would you?' Then he added: 'He is just fourteen today!'

The Kid was terribly bashful.

'All right, then. Him and no more,' said Lizzy hoarsely.

'I don't want to,' said the Kid quietly.

'Don't be daft,' Mylord exhorted him.

'Such an opportunity, you silly little mug,' said Woodpecker loftily.

'Sure,' said Tramp. 'Such an opportunity!'

'But I don't want to,' repeated the Kid.

And then, while he undressed and pulled himself up on to the bunk and breathed heavily, Woodpecker, Mylord, Tramp and the others called out to him in encouragement.

And the Kid did not even notice that Lizzy had not stopped humming.

Afterwards, she went out into the corridor to have a wash.

'Don't make a noise,' Woodpecker warned her.

Then they sat her in their midst, feeling very masculine as they embraced her with a proprietary air which they had just earned the right to adopt, and they sang about the nunnery and the skates.

Lizzy stroked the Kid's head.

Then she combed his hair, and no one laughed to see it.

'Shall I see you home?' asked Woodpecker. 'We're going to pack.' Then he added: 'We got these things ready for you before you came.'

And they began to fill her pockets with all sorts of commodities.

'We couldn't take it with us, anyway,' murmured Woodpecker. 'So why let someone else grab it?'

The things included towels, combs, hair-brushes, and various odds and ends such as darning requisites and jars. At first she tried to refuse, but then she took everything they gave her.

When she was downstairs, they threw a fine quilt after her.

'That is from the Kid,' chuckled Woodpecker.

'Thanks!' she called.

'Bye-bye, Liz!'

'See you!' she replied.

And as she went home, loaded with the boys' gifts, she felt just as sad as she had before, when Woodpecker called for her.

10

'Well, Kid,' said Woodpecker harshly, 'didn't kill you, did it?'

The Kid bowed his head. Taking a pencil out of his knapsack, he began to scribble a postcard to his parents.

'You can sleep with me tonight,' continued Woodpecker. 'One blanket will do for us both.'

'Why did you have to throw just his woollen one after Liz?' Mylord asked him.

'Well, he had to pay something, didn't he?'

'Let me alone,' spoke up the Kid. 'I don't mind.'

He sat on the stool and wrote.

Woodpecker and Mylord left to say good-bye at L 410.

The others also disappeared, and the Kid was left all by himself.

Dear parents, he wrote, *we're leaving for somewhere, but please don't worry, I am grown-up now.*

He counted the words: fourteen. Almost half the permitted number.

They call me Kid and everyone is nice to me.

That was twenty-four. Another six to go.

I'll write again as soon as possible.

He crossed out 'as soon as possible', writing only 'soon' instead, and signed his name.

For a time he just sat there as if carved out of wood.

Then he carried the card out into the corridor and pushed it into the letter-box.

But he did not come back.

First he stood a long while next to the letter-box, and then huddled himself in a corner against the wall, wishing it had not happened; or that he might be going somewhere else than with Woodpecker, Tramp, Mylord, and the others; that it was many, many years later; or that they were all dead; or at least that he himself was dead.

The wall was cold and grey. Someone had scratched all kinds of hieroglyphics on it. Why did they all say he was grown-up now? What was it that had changed? Was that all it was? He gazed into the bowl of the sink on the wall, the disappointment he felt darker than night. And his parents were far, far away. His mother. A cramp took hold of him. The slippery white basin fascinated him. Then he began to vomit.

II

The servant waited for Liselotte until nine. When he had returned the first time to report no success and Marmulstaub had ordered him to go back and bring her even if he had to wait till midnight, all thoughts of tasting his master's tit-bit for himself left him.

'Find out immediately where she is!' said Marmulstaub angrily.

That was something his servant was unable to do. None of the women who lived in the same room with Liselotte knew where she was to be found.

'You can't wait for her here,' they said. 'This is a woman's dormitory.'

He felt too embarrassed to put any more questions to them and he could not explain anything. Marmulstaub would never forgive him if he did that.

So he settled down in the corridor and waited. The tower clock chimed the half-hour. Half-past nine.

No one appeared in the corridor all this time, only an old woman, unable to sleep, had once walked past.

'Shameless creature!' she spat at him. 'Don't you know what's in store for us?'

Completely taken aback, he gasped for breath. The old woman judged him with a glassy stare.

Then all was silence. The clock chimed ten. At that moment he saw the girl.

'Where have you been all this time?' he called in a muted voice. 'You're not allowed out after eight, and my master is waiting for you.'

'Your master?' she asked in surprise. 'Who's that?'

'Mr Marmulstaub,' he said.

'Your master can kiss my backside,' she blurted out.

With a somewhat weary agility she opened the door with her elbow.

'Couldn't you lend a hand?' she suggested.

The servant held the door for her.

Liselotte threw the things she had brought with her under her bed. Relieved, she unmade the bed, not intending to go out any more.

L

The servant stood in the open doorway, appraising her with his eyes.

She paid not the slightest attention to him now, and climbed into bed.

This roused him to anger.

'I'll give him your message, woman,' he muttered, enraged, the first words that came into his head. 'But on your own head be it!'

She made no reply. With a tired but at the same time determined gesture she pulled the blanket right up to her throat.

'Well?' whispered the servant.

'And you too!' she flung at him.

'What!' he said in a raised voice. 'You vessel of impudence.'

'Be quiet!' hissed someone.

'Unheard of!' added the servant as he closed the door carefully behind him.

He had seen the uselessness of his efforts already at nine o'clock. Now he walked back wondering fearfully whether it would be enough to say – if someone stopped him in the street – that he had not been out on his own behalf, but upon the order of the new deputy chairman of the Council of Elders, Ignatz Marmulstaub.

Mouse-like, he crept along the house walls.

Luckily no one saw him. The ghetto was asleep.

12

'Go to bed,' said Marmulstaub sleepily. 'It's official business, and we'll settle it tomorrow.'

But he himself could not go to sleep. Although he tried hard to direct his thoughts to Liselotte or at least to the lost list of defects, something impelled him to dwell on the events of the afternoon. There in the darkness in front of him he saw, like a pair of ghosts, the SS uniforms of Herr von Holler and his second-in-command. And then he saw Löwenbach. In his imagination he was stifled by the dungeon in the cellar. Where

could he only have lost that list? In his mind's eye he also
saw the small queer man in civilian dress who had accompanied the commandant the day before yesterday. Why did
Herr von Holler wait for him last night? Did he perhaps want
to take him down to see Löwenbach? He felt his forehead.
He was sure he had a temperature. His pulse was racing. And
his heart. What was he afraid of, he asked himself, why was
he afraid? He must not breathe so loud. The sound of his own
breathing frightened him. Heavily he rolled over on the bed.
With the palm of one hand he wiped his forehead and both
cheeks. He swallowed with difficulty. He had pulled out his
handkerchief several times during the afternoon, it occurred
to him. And in the carriage he had even taken his jacket off.
Yes, that was it, in the carriage! Before that tall, gangling
lout threw that word in his face. He was suddenly firmly convinced that he had seen the blue envelope with the folded
octavo sheets lying on the purple seat. He concentrated on this
thought with a physical effort, and felt perspiration ooze out
all over his body and his pulse pumping crazily. Confused, he
swallowed whole mouthfuls of saliva. He mustn't give in to the
fever. But the more he thought about it, the more certain he
was that he really had left the list there. And since that
afternoon interview with Herr von Holler forced its way to the
forefront of his consciousness, he conceived the idea of linking
his tour of inspection with his own intention to take a look
at the shop where they were repairing the carriage, at the faded
and torn purple of the seat, or to make inquiries of whoever
was repairing it. But he was unable to make that the focal
point of his thoughts. Still he saw his signature, even if illeg-
ible, on the list from which the transport was to be assembled.
Why had Löwenbach not signed the thing? Again he wiped the
sweat off his face. He ought to have known that he could not
put himself up as an obstacle in the path of such a man as von
Holler. If for nothing else – if for nothing else! – he deserved
to be punished. Fool. Why didn't he see that himself? For
Marmulstaub had exonerated him in every other respect.

13

'Nobody's going anywhere,' said Woodpecker at eight in the morning. 'I asked downstairs. It was all a lot of tattle.'

His way took him past the fence, on the other side of which two gendarmes were going on duty. They looked familiar to him, but he did not realize that he had seen them the day before in the square. The taller one bent down to the other and was speaking away at him. Woodpecker did not even turn to look after them. He only saw that they entered the gate of the German *commandatur*. What might they want there, he wondered idly, but then he forgot all about them.

So nothing had happened.

Just a panic, that was all.

But there was yesterday. Remember, how he had got out of repairing that carriage? And Lizzy and the Kid. And there had been something in the air, something that said that nothing mattered; that he need not fear anything. At least inside him, right inside. An experience, a real experience for life, as Tramp was fond of saying.

Yesterday's ditty about the skates and the nunnery came into his head.

Tam-ta, tam-ta, tam . . .

He could not get rid of it, its every note conjuring up for him a picture of yesterday's evening with all the details of their leave-taking at 410. But over and above all those moments before it.

He began to imagine how next Thursday the wild melodies would again come pouring out of the silver cornets of their trumpets.

That was life.

One day life was going to be just that and nothing else.

The workshop welcomed him with the grey pounding of hammers and the bluish hissing of flames above the black-smith's bellows. He put on his leather apron, thinking disgustedly that he had in front of him an entire afternoon on that wretched carriage.

'Good thing you are here,' the blacksmith greeted him. 'That's it, don't give way to panic. Have you heard the whispers up your way?'

'I should say so,' replied Woodpecker.

'Well, it's possible, my boy,' added the blacksmith, speaking more quietly, 'that it's going to be said out loud. And that it will be true. But even then we'll not fall on our arses.'

'I couldn't care less if we do go,' said Woodpecker as he laid both the axles of the coach on the ground in front of him. 'At least I'll get to know something new.'

'That's what I say, lad. It seems to me you know a thing or two already – such as girls – or perhaps a good feed?'

'Not that,' said Woodpecker, going red in the face. Did they perhaps know about Lizzy, he wondered.

'Here, take a look at this, you scamp,' said the blacksmith quietly.

Woodpecker glanced at the paper the other held out to him, and in the relief which he immediately felt he almost blurted out that that was nothing, that he had the same or something very similar at home, and that it was his duty to pass it on to someone else just as the blacksmith himself was doing. And that his paper said exactly the same thing – that the Allies were giving the Germans a thrashing. He breathed a sigh of relief. Nothing about Lizzy then.

'What does it say?' he asked, and read perfunctorily: 'Death to the Fascists . . .' Then his voice fell, with disappointment as much as relief, and he looked at the blacksmith. 'I know this.'

'Hide it,' murmured the blacksmith, adding: 'Well, I must run along, lad. Let me know, won't you.'

'Sure,' Woodpecker said with a laugh, patting the pocket into which he had thrust the leaflet.

He lit the fire, and as he pumped the bellows he watched the bluish flames swell up into the air and to either side. His mind was fully occupied elsewhere – there was yesterday, and now there was this leaflet, all of it rousing in him the notion that somewhere behind a barrier there was life waiting for him and putting out its tentacles to reach at him with these events. His fantasies found form in the flickering flames.

'Well, lads,' said the blacksmith when he came back a few moments later, 'there's no mistake about it: the old gentleman, Mr Löwenbach, hasn't come back. Something's up. Maybe a transport.'

And he left again immediately.

'He's going to scout round for news,' muttered the other blacksmith, who was usually in charge of the workshop in his absence, 'until . . .'

Woodpecker waited, curious to know what the blacksmith was going to say.

But the other was silent, while Woodpecker reflected that the whole thing was probably not so terribly serious. Again he saw everything in the fire: Lizzy, pressing Mylord's hand. And the Kid, crouching on his stool and writing. Yesterday seemed to disappear in the transparent flames which now held a bluish promise of better things to come: everything would change when Russia and England with America defeated Germany and Lizzy would walk along the street with her children and nobody would stop her. And the Kid would ride a junior bicycle and his parents would wrap him up in cotton-wool because they wouldn't know any better.

He raised his eyes. Rot, he thought. Nothing but dreams. Better think about getting Lizzy to come to number 20 again one of these days.

14

The doors of the blacksmith's shop flew open violently.

'Attention!' shouted the blacksmith, who was standing by the door, with great presence of mind.

Englebert von Holler, SS, and his civilian companion

entered the workshop, all of whose occupants tensed expectantly.

'Stand easy! Carry on work!' said the commandant.

The first thing that came into Woodpecker's mind was to put his hand in his pocket and throw the leaflet in the flames. But before he could move, two other SS men and the two gendarmes, the tall one and the small one, whom he had met that morning, came into the shop. Damn, said Woodpecker to himself. What a mess!

The taller of the two gendarmes took up a position directly behind Woodpecker. He instantly recognized the loud-mouthed boy of yesterday afternoon, and again felt an urge to box his ears. Just like that, more in a fatherly fashion now than anything else. Yesterday he could not have imagined the tanned hooligan in a leather blacksmith's apron such as the one he had on now, standing there so strangely silent.

'Where's the foreman?' asked the commandant, without much interest.

'I am substituting for him,' said the blacksmith. 'He's working outside.' Scouting round for news, that was what he was doing, he thought. And certainly a damn sight luckier than he was even though he was so very careful about everything.

'Stop that hammering!' shouted the small man beside Herr von Holler.

The workshop grew quiet, and Woodpecker wondered how this would end. All of a sudden he saw it all as a sporting event, though to be frank it didn't look too good. It didn't look good at all. A proper jam. Because he had that thing in his pocket and was unable to take it out and throw it away unobserved.

'Are you working on anything for us?' the commandant asked.

'Yes, Herr General,' replied the blacksmith. 'The fittings for the door of your Mercedes.'

'I'm not a general, idiot! Don't you know the badges of rank?'

'No,' stammered the blacksmith.

'What else?'

'Nothing – only the carriage . . . for Herr Marmulstaub.'

'What carriage?'

'A creaking one, sir,' faltered the blacksmith. But he did did not mean it as a joke.

'Who is repairing it?'

'Woodpecker . . . I mean Mahler, sir.'

'Stand aside! Woodpecker-Mahler to me!'

Woodpecker came up to him as slowly as he could. This is bad, he kept repeating to himself. This is bad. Although the distance separating him from the commandant was small, he shuffled along for what seemed to be a very long time. He had paled slightly, for it had occurred to him what the possible consequences might be. You are in a pretty pickle, lad, he seemed to hear the foreman say.

The small man standing beside the commandant cast a severe look at the tall gendarme behind Woodpecker. He understood at once what was expected of him, and he prodded the boy. He can take that in place of the box on the ears, he thought irritably, saying out loud:

'Get a move on!'

Herr von Holler had in the meantime turned to the small fellow.

'They're shaking like leaves in the wind. You can see for yourself. We have long ago liquidated the pigsty of tolerance here,' he said with satisfaction in his voice. (Perhaps the tiny idiot had heard something about that already, he reflected.)

'Are you sure?' queried the small one.

'I think so,' replied the commandant nonchalantly, thinking of the ruin that was Löwenbach last night and of the astonishment shown by the half-pint of a man at his elbow, who had after all not expected such an interrogation.

15

Woodpecker saw only the pair of eyes on a level with his face, the strangest eyes he had ever seen. They were narrow, green, all-knowing and able to look inside you. He also noticed the thin straight nose with nostrils slightly distended and overgrown with thick black hairs, as well as the ginger moustache above the compressed lips. But the muscular and sinewy face of the commandant escaped him, it seemed completely alien and incomprehensible. So this was his enemy. But he did not know as yet in what way they were to fight.

Herr von Holler held his short, silver-and-diamond-studded cane in a gloved hand. It shone, casting a dazzling aurora around it.

'Mahler?' he inquired.

'Yes,' nodded Woodpecker.

'Who is this brat that he swaggers like this?' demanded the courier, though he saw quite clearly that the boy was far from swaggering – he was merely much taller. As soon as he heard the man's words, he bent his knees a little to make himself appear smaller.

'Would you mind lending me this?' asked the small man, pointing to the commandant's cane. Then he took it, gave a slight leap, and hit Woodpecker on the forehead.

'There, that's it,' he said when Woodpecker bent farther still.

'Excuse me,' said Herr von Holler, taking back his cane.

The boy's eyes wandered helplessly around the workshop. He had known this would happen, so what was he so surprised about, he reflected. He would pretend that it hurt him more than it actually did. Even so, he was in a mess. God, if Tramp or Mylord or the blacksmith could see him now! He must crouch down a bit more so as not to rile that titch of a fellow any more than necessary. Then they might think he was afraid, and would not search his pockets. On the other hand it occurred to him, that was just the sort of thing they did. Well, he must be on his toes and wait.

The courier's eyes bored into him.

'What has he got on him?' he asked, but the question sounded as if it were addressed to the commandant.

'Do you smoke?' asked Herr von Holler, pretending not to

notice the little man and looking as if the whole affair was beginning to amuse him.

'No,' said Woodpecker.

'Turn your pockets out,' the commandant ordered him. 'It'll be too bad for you if I find the least scrap of tobacco!' And, turning to the courier, he added: 'Tobacco, that's my speciality.'

'You won't,' said Woodpecker insolently.

'Take out everything,' continued the commandant, 'and turn them inside out.'

So here it was, thought Woodpecker, this was it. As bad as he had imagined it would be. How was he to get out of this jam, how was he to fool them? Slowly he began to empty his pockets, turning round as he did so to prevent the commandant from seeing that he was leaving one pocket out. The fight was on. He would have to keep his wits about him if he was to get the better of those two. Or else it was going to be even worse than he had expected. Good job he had the apron on, he could at least pretend that it was difficult to get at the pockets.

'It seems that he doesn't smoke,' said the commandant, amused.

'This one too!' barked the courier, and ripped the boy's apron off.

Woodpecker had kept his hand there too long. He saw now that he was losing the contest. With exaggerated slowness he pulled out his handkerchief. Or perhaps it was not so slow, after all. The whole thing seemed to him – certainly at this moment – more like a game of hide-and-seek. Then he took out his penknife and a lump of sugar he had brought for his elevenses.

'Well . . .' said the commandant.

'He's got something there,' snapped the courier.

'Let's have a look,' said Herr von Holler, and put his hand in the boy's pocket.

Woodpecker went deathly pale. It struck him suddenly that this was no game, nor had it been right from the start. He was for it now and no mistake. With everything included, and he had heard of the things they did to people. He was not likely to go home now, and, who knew, perhaps he would never go anywhere again. Perhaps, also, not even a fraction would come true of everything he had thought about such a short and yet such a long while ago – over the blue flames.

Herr von Holler unfolded the sheet of paper he had extracted from Woodpecker's pocket. His expression changed.

'So,' he said as he passed the leaflet to the courier, 'this kind of thing is being carried around here! After all my precautionary measures. Very well.'

'Filth!' muttered the other after a moment, his small pig's eyes glowing with excitement.

Woodpecker now felt the eyes of all upon himself. The foreman was out. What was he to say, he wondered, when they asked him, as they were sure to do straightaway. He'd say something, but not the truth. *Just something.*

'Where did you get this?'

Here it was. They were asking already. Must he reply at once? His eyes searched the ground.

That bloody fool, Marmulstaub, Herr von Holler swore to himself. Why the hell did he have to drag him here of all places?

'Well? Why don't you speak?'

'I don't know,' said Woodpecker.

'How did you get hold of it?' hissed the courier. He leaped up and hit the boy in the face with his fist.

And then he was showered by blows from both of the men standing in front of him.

Suddenly it all seemed silly to him. He could not possibly tell them, surely they must see that for themselves. He just did not know. That was all the answer he could give them. They had no sense of fair play. He ducked a blow only to get another from the other side. (Now a tooth fell out.) If he acted differently, he thought, it would be a dirty thing to do. That brought him to the end of this chain of thought. There was no more to it, nothing more to be said. Perhaps they were going to beat him good and proper, he told himself, and then some more. And not only here and now. There were still the SS men and the gendarmes. But not even then could he blab. Well, could he? He could take it all right, he told himself (and swallowed a second tooth). After all, they could not beat him for ever. They would get tired in time. But he would not. He could take more. Maybe he would soon stop feeling the blows even.

Then he was conscious only of the orange glow from the commandant's ring every time the fist came near his face. He was not going to blab, he thought once more, wearily. What would the foreman say if he did?

'Perhaps this will loosen your tongue,' he heard Herr von Holler say menacingly.

Woodpecker saw a pistol in the commandant's hand. Well, the game was up, he told himself with finality. The game was up, and he had lost. Without being really aware of it, he clenched his teeth.

'Now will you talk, you bastard!' hissed the little man.

'Talk!' yelled Herr von Holler.

16

Marmulstaub puffed as he searched the smithy yard with his dark-purple gaze. At last he caught sight of his carriage, its wheels gone because Woodpecker had taken the axles into the workshop. With short steps he hurried to the carriage, feeling pleased both that he had brought the commandant here and that he would not have to climb up high. What was there that Herr von Holler could find amiss here? Nothing. On the contrary, Marmulstaub thought contentedly, here they were working for his garages! Clumsily he clambered up on to the box. Once there, he saw the foreman on the other side, well concealed from sight and pretending to be examining the creaking springs.

'What're you doing here, man?'

'Mending your coach, dear sir,' replied the blacksmith, irritated that the frog should be nosing about just here. He had seen him arrive with the commandant, but Marmulstaub had left him as the armed SS men entered the workshop. The blacksmith's anxiety about the boy in the smithy was transformed in the course of his conversation with the fat man into a blind fury. 'What business is it of yours, anyway? What're you looking for? Or are you a Nazi too?'

Marmulstaub ignored this outburst with the calmness of condescension. He did not even raise his eyes. 'My carriage,' he said. 'All right. Didn't you by any chance find a blue envelope here?'

'No,' replied the foreman, gazing questioningly into Marmulstaub's dark-blue eyes.

'You are an insolent fellow,' said Marmulstaub.

It suddenly struck the blacksmith that if the fat man was really looking for his envelope, this was an opportunity to call the boy out from the workshop.

'I'm sorry,' he said quickly. 'I'm a little nervous.'

'Forget it,' said Marmulstaub, and he climbed heavily to the other side. For forgetfulness, he thought, was the burying place of human folly in which all our words and deeds were interred. With his small white hands he explored the purple seat right at the back.

'Somebody else was working here yesterday,' said the foreman. 'You can call him and ask him yourself.'

The fat man suddenly seemed to change in his eyes, he seemed kind and almost gentle. And his word, thought the blacksmith, carried a lot of weight with the commandant. He implored him with a gaze.

'Who?' asked Marmulstaub. He could see that the other man was badly shaken by something.

'Ask for Woodpecker,' came the eager reply. 'He's there with them – in the workshop.'

Marmulstaub climbed down without saying anything. He pulled his coat straight and cleaned his shoes. Then he dis-

appeared behind the smithy door, and the foreman again hid
behind the coach.

17

'Marmulstaub!' shouted the commandant as soon as the
fat man entered. It was the second time that he had raised his
voice. 'You idiot! Where have you taken us?'

'Excellency . . .'

'Where have you brought us, you bloody ass? This is the
limit! We are doing our best for you – a coffee-house, and
Catholic services on Sundays. Hostels for the children and
music for the whores. And the lousy rebels' nest is not even
being shelled. This is mutiny! Here, you read it!'

Marmulstaub caught the leaflet as it was thrown to him.

Then he noticed the boy, realizing in spite of his fear and
confusion that it was the hooligan who had insulted him the
day before. It was a wonder he had recognized him, though,
seeing that the boy was bloody all over. So I've not escaped
it, thought Marmulstaub, only it is the boy instead of Löwenbach. He was still standing in front of the commandant in an
extremely uncomfortable posture, bent almost double.

'I wouldn't give it to him, if I were you,' said the little man
in a quiet, irritated voice. 'You are taking him too much into
your confidence.'

The commandant threw Marmulstaub an ominous look.

Marmulstaub remained as he was, undecided whether to
read the leaflet or not.

The courier spat in front of him.

The fat man automatically took a step backwards. The
commandant's greenish-grey uniform with the silver epaulettes
and the black skull and cross-bones on the cap terrified him.
His condition was aggravated by the sleepless night he had
spent, by the suspense in which he had been until that moment
of relaxation a little while ago, by the sight of the boy, and the
diamonds on the commandant's cane, as well as by the pistol
in his other hand.

'It is impudent,' he said humbly. 'I can only say, Excellency . . .'

Horrified, he looked at the boy and blinked his eyes. Why had this happened? After all, he had forgiven him that word.

'I have finished with you, Marmulstaub!' said the commandant. 'The transport will leave tomorrow. You will put it together right now, from that rag you signed in place of Löwenbach.' In the eyes of the fat man he saw an unspoken question. 'Where to? You'll find out! Blockhead!'

'Excellency . . .'

'Don't gabble! You'll go with them, you bloody fool, you idiot! You can piece Löwenbach together on the way. And tell this one to talk, or you'll be taking his corpse along tomorrow!'

'Yes, Excellency,' whispered Marmulstaub.

But as he turned obediently towards the boy to urge him to speak, he saw in his eyes a glow that frightened him.

Woodpecker had suddenly begun to hate them all; the tiny man who had to spring up at him whenever he wished to hit him in the face, preferring therefore to beat him about the hips and thighs instead, and Herr von Holler, who had looked so mild at first, and the fat frog because he trembled and kept quiet. Woodpecker's hate now included even the foreman, who was the only one lucky enough to leave the smithy in time. All of a sudden the commandant lost his knotty and sinewy incomprehensibility. Everything around Woodpecker – the commandant's face and the faces of the others – merged into something beast-like, something that bore but a faint and almost imperceptible resemblance to human countenances. He was seized by a desperate longing to return their blows, and his eyes sought that familiar piece of metal, the carriage axle he had been repairing.

And still Marmulstaub did not speak.

'Speak up, or I'll kill you!' threatened the commandant. 'Who wrote it?'

'I did!' shouted Woodpecker wildly, his eyes having found the axle. 'And Russia!'

He jumped for the iron rod, bent down to the ground, and then straightened up again (he could not tell whether it took him long or not). He began furiously to wave the axle and thresh all around him, blindly, for he could not see for blood. At first his eyes misted only gradually, but then the scene in front of him seemed to dissolve into darkness and he saw nothing any more. He heard a shot, then another. He closed his eyes. Opening them once more, he felt he could almost see the sharp points which penetrated his chest in a countless number of places, and he forced himself to keep his eyes open a little longer. Grasping the axle more firmly in his hands (it was indescribably heavy now, yet at the same time it seemed without any weight at all) he struck with it where he thought he saw the commandant's cap.

Marmulstaub groaned. He had expected the second and third shots to be directed at him.

Both, however, ploughed into the body of the boy.

18

Just before eleven both the gendarmes, the tall and the small one, reported to Herr von Holler, who had a bandage on his head.

'Take both of them to the trucks!'

The cellar into which they had to descend to carry out the order was dark and filled with a heavy stench. Rats scurried about under their trouser legs.

'Out, quickly!' said the taller gendarme, and caught hold of Löwenbach's arm.

'I can't,' he whispered.

'You must!' said the gendarme.

The smaller gendarme pushed his helmet to the back of his head and supported fat Ignatz Marmulstaub.

'Thank you,' said Marmulstaub hoarsely.

'All right, come along!' said the small gendarme when they were outside.

In a few moments they were marching through the ghetto, a strange procession before which people stood aside, unwittingly forming a line on either side of the street.

On the left side, where Marmulstaub walked with downcast eyes, the people began to spit demonstratively, muttering among themselves in a menacing rumble. In their invective they, however, refrained from gesticulating, afraid that such gestures might be mistakenly thought by the gendarmes to be meant for them.

On the right side, where the taller gendarme half-dragged the pitiful wreck of a man, the pair was accompanied by commiserating glances.

They arrived at the 'big-wigs'' house in which both of them lived. Although it was in contravention of Herr von Holler's orders, he having commanded that the two men be taken directly to the train, the gendarmes allowed them to go up to wash and change.

They waited outside, promenading up and down the pavement in front of the house.

'Hot, isn't it?' said the taller gendarme, his Adam's apple jumping wildly up and down his throat. 'As bad as yesterday.'

'It's been like this for almost a week now,' replied the smaller gendarme. 'How about going to the river this afternoon?'

Just at that moment the crowd which had gathered in the street made a dash for the house.

'Out, all of you!' shouted the tall gendarme. He managed to chase most of the intruders out.

'Have you gone crazy?' the smaller gendarme upbraided them as he waved others back from the staircase and through the passage into the street.

At last they succeeded in driving out all who had no business to be in the house, a small woman with a vividly painted face being the last to go. Marmulstaub was sitting on the floor, weeping and groaning.

'Come on, get up,' said the taller gendarme.

'Thank you,' said Marmulstaub hoarsely.

M

The tall gendarme nodded to his companion, indicating that it was time they were going.

Out in the street once more, he bent down to the smaller gendarme. 'This bloody heat!' he said in a strangled voice.

'I don't mind it,' replied the other wearily, pushing his helmet back from his forehead.

Soon they reached the railway station.

The Ghettoswingers band stood assembled by the side of the train. They began to play, at a word of command from Herr von Holler, just at the moment when two SS men accompanied by the little man from Berlin were throwing Woodpecker's canvas-shrouded body into the last cattle-truck; They did not shut the truck's sliding-door until David Löwenbach and Ignatz Marmulstaub had got in.

The trumpets screamed. Mylord pressed the mouthpiece to lips which were completely devoid of blood. The saxophones wailed a familiar melody:

> We are becoming sea-sick,
> An ill-fated crew are we.

Hope

SIMON stopped at the foot of the stone staircase. The stairs exuded the chillness of the earth and the greyish reflection of the rainy day. Only a few moments ago he had assured himself that it was unnecessary to keep watch today, since the curfew was still in force. We're not allowed out, he kept saying to himself, and so no one will come in, either. But then he caught sight of Chana's eyes. He cast a quick, distrustful look at the figure of the old Jew from Essen, sitting there all hunched up as if to keep out the cold. And since it was his turn today, he at last picked himself up and went out.

He sat down underneath the small roof made out of old crates. His body moved every time he breathed, filling his lungs with the sharp, malodorous after-taste of excrement and lime. His throat was constricted. He rocked automatically backwards and forwards and from side to side as though trying to extricate himself and to avoid the streaming rain. This movement told him that he was still capable of something – that he was capable of more than just sitting still. However, he was glad that nobody else knew about it: they couldn't ask more of him than of the old man from Essen. And yet, on the other hand, he longed to be able to let someone into the secret of his strength, and to have it appreciated.

Even now, when everything was deadened by the rain, the pungent smell of the courtyard seemed to him to be hostile. He must not move about so much. He counted how many more times he would have to come out here . . . three or perhaps five. But he would have to come down in any case, even if it were not for this . . . When he added together everything that seemed good to him, he again had that feeling which he had already experienced yesterday, the feeling that

195

because of what he, in his mediocrity, had found, he would witness something that he could not quite comprehend, though it was within his reach, in a misty sort of way. He yearned for it, but at the same time he was afraid to think about it in case it vanished as soon as he got to the bottom of it.

Heedless of the rain which ran down his face, he looked up. He saw the tall buildings, overgrown with wilted ivy on greenish walls covered with copper-coloured and greenish mould. Somehow this house reminded him of the past.

Here and there a bluish crystal of light flickered through the rain. He inclined his head to one side. Soon he felt the damp even through his coat. It was too worn, it occurred to him, and he felt a constricting pity. But then he thought how lucky he was to have a coat at all – those up there, where an invisible cloud concealed everything that would probably take place tonight, or perhaps not till tomorrow, did not even have that. He crouched on his seat, watching the grey mass of cloud, which looked like dark, wet shadows. He still did not feel cold enough to have to leave. Crossing his arms over his chest, he kept his body as warm as he could.

A poster hung on the wall of the latrine:

> *Nicht vergessen*
> *vor dem Essen . . .*
> *die Hände waschen!*

He stared for a moment at the black type. Then he tired of it. His eyes wandered over the glistening puddles. To anyone watching, it might have seemed that his eyesight was poor, for he suddenly started to rub his eyes with the backs of both hands. Or it might have seemed that he was crying. But Simon was not crying.

He walked away, going right through the middle of a puddle that had grown larger in the persistent downpour.

'You're back already?' Chana asked him in surprise.

'Don't worry,' he replied. 'Nobody's going to steal that dirty kennel.'

'Come and sit down,' she said, adding: 'Why, you're wet through, Simon. Don't you want to take your things off?'

'Aren't you cold?' she asked finally.

He was tired, and so he did not reply.

He would have liked to strip everything off because the coat chilled him, but he sat down on the mattress as he was. For a moment he sat there, looking at Chana's hair. Fifty-two years ago, he reckoned in his mind, she had a small and bright black knot. That was the fashion in those days. He must not think of the cold so much, he said to himself.

'I'm not saying anything,' she remarked after a while, seeing that he still did not make any reply but just sat, watching the water dripping from the tails of his coat to the floor. She was anxious in case anyone should scold him for not keeping watch outside, since it was his turn.

Simon was fully occupied with his thoughts. When he was close to Chana he always felt he was wronging her. He stroked her hair with a short, quick gesture. He felt as though he were saying good-bye. He narrowed his eyes in order to see only the dim outlines of the fancies that were carried along, gossamer-like, on waves of thought based on his past life to somewhere in the future where no one could see. He was unable to tell her about this, yet equally unable to escape his imaginings.

He rose. 'I must go down, anyway,' he said at last.

And then he added: 'But not for that.'

'I know,' she replied. But it took her some time before she understood.

Downstairs, Simon passed the wall with the poster hanging on it without looking at it. His coat was completely wet through by now and it chilled him more and more.

The black and yellow colours underneath the skull and cross-bones – the symbol of typhus – shattered his deliberate nonchalance. Good job I didn't undress, he said to himself. He looked away, and stretched his hands out to the rain. Now, he thought, I am clean and safe again. But what if it stopped raining? The poster suddenly seemed to come to life – where-ever Simon turned, he always saw the rain-soaked paper in front of him. He shivered. Then he turned and went in.

With considerable difficulty he withdrew his feet, wrapped in rags, from the rough, knotty sabots, which he found to be full of sticky mud. At any rate he could still stand quite a lot – he could, if need be, walk about like this for as long as an hour.

Dragging himself upstairs to Chana he breathed heavily and rapidly.

'Come and sit right by me,' she said. 'That'll warm you up.'

'I got very wet in the rain,' he remarked.

'Doesn't matter,' she comforted him, and involuntarily moved a little to the side.

'Thanks,' he said. 'It's raining heavily today.'

'It rained yesterday, too,' she said. Then she took his numb hands in hers.

'Quiet there!' called out Mother Cohen, who was lying by the wall on the opposite side of the room. 'We're still sleeping.'

'We can talk, can't we,' Simon said angrily. 'I've been down twice already!'

Without saying anything he borrowed Chana's shawl and wound it round his waist. He felt a sharp twinge in the spot where his kidneys were. Never mind, he thought, something is bound to hurt when you are old. Well, in this case it was the kidneys. It was a single stab of pain each time, and it started first thing in the morning.

Simon's neighbour on the left, a desiccated Jew from Essen, who had amused himself all evening yesterday by counting the inhabitants of the house, now got up and stood by Simon's mattress, shifting from one foot to the other. But Simon did not say a word.

Suddenly the man from Essen caught sight of the puddle that had formed under the tails of Simon's coat.

'Ah!' he said. 'It's raining, is it?'

Then, with a quick movement, he snatched the strong, gold-rimmed glasses from his nose and raised his arm, blinking his eyes short-sightedly as he did so.

'I'll exchange them,' he said excitedly, 'for bread.'

'But, man,' Chana replied, 'you won't be able to see if you do.'

'And what is there for me to see, can you tell me?' the old man demanded irritably. 'What should I look at? You perhaps?'

Simon started.

The man from Essen began to sob, strangely and convulsively, gazing all the while at the puddle by Simon's mattress. Then he interspersed his sobbing with disjointed, incoherent words. As he did not understand a single one of them, Simon did not think it necessary to comfort the old Jew from Essen.

'Oh, heavens,' said Mother Cohen, 'it's impossible to sleep in this place.'

'Why do you keep grouching, then?' said Simon sarcastically.

'And anyway, it's morning already.'

'Men shouldn't cry,' said Mother Cohen all of a sudden.

'No, they shouldn't,' Simon agreed.

'I'm talking to your wife,' retorted Mother Cohen.

'Simon isn't mangy,' protested Chana.

'Did I say he was?' asked Mother Cohen.

'He was down for the second time a while ago,' added Chana. 'And he got wet through.'

'But he doesn't cry,' said Mother Cohen.

'Stop crying!' said Simon, turning to the Jew from Essen. They could not accustom themselves to the unusual sound of a man crying.

'They're all like that in Germany,' said Mother Cohen, 'either they shoot or they cry.'

Then she added: 'Either you're doing some silly counting or you worry your head off.'

'He isn't crying any more,' said Simon.

'I wasn't crying,' the man from Essen claimed.

'You were,' Simon insisted.

'Leave him be,' said Chana.

'Don't argue!' shouted Mother Cohen.

'What's the matter with you?' asked Chana, surprised.
'What are you getting so excited about?'

'Hm,' said Mother Cohen. And then: 'My son arrived yesterday.'

'Your son?' queried Simon. 'You have a son?'

'Yes,' she said.

'How old is he?'

'Forty.'

'He is still young,' said Simon.

'He'll still be able to find something, if he survives,' added
Chana.

The idea came to Simon suddenly that there were still
people who had a son, and that they were in fact younger
through having somebody. They, Chana and he, had no one,
it occurred to him. Only he had those fancies of his. And
that, come to think of it, was perhaps even better, because
Mother Cohen's son might leave or something might happen
to him, whereas he could keep his fancies whatever happened.

'You must be glad . . .' said Chana.

'I don't know,' replied Mother Cohen. 'I've been expecting
him.'

'Well, you got your wish,' said Simon.

'That's just the point,' remarked Mother Cohen.

Simon understood – it should not have happened. But none
of this should have happened to any of them. And he thought,
'She should have told us yesterday already.'

The flat-bottomed funeral cart arrived at noon. Somebody
had cut off the wooden ornaments and knocked away the
baldachin on its slim, gilded pillars. The cart brought food
and medicines.

A blond cook, about eighteen years old, exposed his bare
chest to the rain, surveying everything from his frog's-eye
view in the courtyard. In a white apron girded with a leather
belt, his arms bare, he wordlessly filled the old men's mess-
tins.

'What have you brought us?' Simon asked him. 'The end of
the war?'

'You don't want much, do you, Grandpa?' the cook retorted.

Simon felt that there was a great deal of contempt in those
words, even after the young fellow produced an extra keg of
groats. But he kept quiet for fear of not getting anything.

'You should give us the extra straightaway,' he muttered.

'Why, you old so-and-so,' said the cook, 'I pinched this
for you at my own risk. And what's more, I could keep it for
myself if I felt like it.' He spat in an arc over the heads of
Simon and the man from Essen.

Simon walked up the stairs to Chana.

'I got some extra for you,' he said.

'Groats with saccharine,' remarked Mother Cohen. 'Fine
things they invented in Germany, I must say.'

'You're a wonder, Simon,' said Chana.

The man from Essen finished his meal first. 'We've invented
other things as well in Germany,' he said. He had put his
glasses on again.

He shouldn't take everything that's said about Germany so
personally, thought Simon.

Nobody said anything.

'We've given Germany all we had,' continued the old man
from Essen. 'In the war even our brains and our blood.'

After a while he added: 'Perhaps that was a mistake.'

All of a sudden Simon recalled everything he had thought
about down there, when he was completely alone and re-
flecting on things that were far away and yet within reach.

'Anyway,' he rebuffed the old man, 'Hitler won't last.'
Strangely enough, he now felt that he had pleased him. He
did not know himself what had made him say it. Even now
he had to admit that this house, and the train which had
brought him and Chana here, and the rails over which the
train had rattled, and the gendarmes who had come to drive
them out of their flat and later out of the trucks, and the
wooden shack which he was to guard from daybreak to night-
fall today — that all this acted as a prop for the man who
was responsible for their being here on these mattresses. Was

this perhaps the fruit of those interminable reflections down there, where he had tried to forget the squabbles and the idle bragging that went on within these four walls, where the frontier between fact and fantasy disappeared, and when he did not have to think all the time of the stabbing pains in his kidneys nor to fear the weariness that he knew would come one day; where, on the contrary, the conviction gathered force that there was in him some power, and also hope, that he, a human being of little account whose death, when it came, would be noticed by no one apart from Chana, still had a lot to learn. Now he looked at his rain-cleansed hand, and started to count off on his fingers all the things he knew and all the things he did not know. And among those that he did not know there was something that was enormous and yet somehow seemed familiar to him.

'And what if he does last?' asked the Jew from Essen. 'What if he wins?'

'He won't,' said Simon, thinking that perhaps he should not just leave it at that. It also occurred to him that the chap from Essen considered himself more a German than a Jew and that injustice perpetrated by the country in which he had been born hurt him more than it did Simon and Chana.

'How could he win?' asked Mother Cohen, both anger and fear sounding in her voice. 'Why do you listen to this nincompoop?' she added.

Chana was silent.

'He's fighting the whole world.'

Simon, all of a sudden, had nothing to say.

'Simon,' said Chana, 'is your coat dry?'

'I think so,' he replied.

Then they were all silent again. He could return to his thoughts of a few moments ago, the thoughts he had had yesterday and every time that there was silence in the room. He knew that he was with Chana and yet a long way away from her. Involuntarily he pressed his hand to his kidneys.

'Do you want your shawl back?' he asked.

'No, I don't,' she replied.

'I'll give it back to you if you want,' he repeated.

'No,' she said, 'I don't want it.' And she thought: He is fighting the whole world – even the heavens.

Simon held her hand. She recalled snatches of conversation that ended in just such a silence. Here, she thought, in this room they had already had a morgue, a church, and a general staff.

Simon was eagerly playing with the tips of his fingers. She could not fail to notice this, as he had let go of her hand. His eyes took on a gleam that frightened her. He was counting the Allies on his fingers. And on the last he saw a country so large that he could not imagine her otherwise than as a bear. He saw her with an inner vision that was manifested outwardly only by the feverish lustre of his eyes – saw her both as a small bear-cub and as an old, angry beast of prey, then as a she-bear determined to protect all her children. Automatically he clenched his hot hands into fists, giving up his count. He had only one wish – that the she-bear should succeed. Staring ahead absent-mindedly, he opened his right hand and gazed at the tip of his little finger.

Chana was frightened. His eyes looked almost inflamed.

'Simon . . .' she began.

Receiving no reply, she repeated his name once more: 'Simon!'

'Leave me alone,' he said.

'Simon, I'm scared.'

'Don't be,' he said.

'But I am, and I don't know why.'

'Don't be,' he repeated.

'I am. For you.'

'Don't be,' he mumbled again.

And again there was silence.

The old man from Essen grew restless.

'Here we are waiting for supper,' he said suddenly, 'and they're not bringing it. That means that either they've left

our house out or they're late. If they've left it out it means
that either the cook was offended because of those groats
or he thinks we've had enough. Then there are again two
possibilities: either he's on his way or he isn't and is taking
time off at our expense. That means . . .'

'Stop it! Mother Cohen interrupted him.

But then she added: 'Come to think of it, it's true. It's
pitch dark outside and supper nowhere. What time is it,
actually?'

'Simon,' said Chana, 'I'm afraid for you.'

'Perhaps he's not coming at all today,' suggested Simon.

'I'm afraid for us,' Chana repeated.

'After all, you've heard that nobody's allowed out today
because someone was seen smoking on the ramparts,' Simon
went on.

'But they came at lunch-time,' said the old man from Essen.

'So they did,' replied Simon. He wanted badly to get back
to those thoughts of his. But Chana would not leave him
alone.

'Let me be,' he said. 'There's nothing the matter with me.'

'Well, at least give me your hand.'

The Jew from Essen looked their way.

'Do you think they'll let us starve to death?' he asked
Simon.

'Surely not,' Simon replied.

'Here?' asked Chana.

She was joined by Mother Cohen, who said: 'I suppose
it's possible that they won't come.'

Simon was listening attentively.

'Wait a minute,' he called out. 'I think there's somebody in
the yard.'

'You should be down there, keeping a look out,' said
Mother Cohen.

'It's raining,' said Chana. 'And it's dark already.'

'Be quiet!' muttered the old Jew from Essen.

'There's nobody there,' said Chana.

'Just the wind,' the old man whispered. And then he went on:

> ' 'Twas just the wind on a barren plain;
> The pilgrim said: "Oh, stay!
> Tell we where thou flyest, brother mine."
> But the mute wind would not say . . ."

'That's nonsense,' said Simon.

'You figure it out for yourself,' the old man replied. 'It's the thirteenth today, and a Friday at that. An unlucky day.'

'Nonsense!' Simon repeated irritably.

Chana started. The old man from Essen began to pray by the wall.

He let go of her hand. He was now whispering through his bloodless lips, repeating the words 'they'll come', fearfully rejecting doubts which occurred to him, posing the question of what would happen if it did not come off. Then again, his eyes half-closed, he would think of something that was a long way ahead of him, something that he could concentrate on only if there was such a silence as this, his thoughts penetrating the darkness on wings of light. His long, bony fingers reminded him of all his fancies, the Allies, and the last, big country shrouded in something that Simon did not understand but in which he neverthless put all his hopes. In it were both courage and fear, it was dark as the coming night and at the same time light as the hope he had had that morning and as the remaining strength that he knew was dormant in him because he could feel it, strength sufficient to allow him to grasp all of it and hold it in his fingers, which until now he had kept stretched open, and to retain it for himself. Now, as he held it out at arm's length, all he wished for was that the she-bear should succeed, because now he saw her only as a mother. He hoped that the people who would come from over there would be like the mother bear of his imagination. And, in order not to wrong them, he now in his heart of hearts removed the question-mark behind what was only a short while ago still a question: whether they would really come. He had never before experienced such a feeling of absolute resignation as now took hold of him. His eyes burned.

The old man's prayer seemed to be never-ending.

But Simon said to himself that it did not matter. With his aged hand he was stroking mother she-bear, feeling her to be quite near to him now and thinking that she had good and wise eyes.

The cart with the evening coffee did not arrive.

'I don't think they'll come,' said Chana.

'They will,' he replied.

'Aren't you hungry, Simon?'

'No, I'm not,' he said.

He was gazing through the window into the rainy night, and through the night towards the distant mountains whose summits were biting into the sky, and farther still.

'They won't come,' said Chana.

'They will,' repeated Simon.

He took her hand.

'I'm afraid they won't come.'

'Don't be afraid,' he reassured her. 'They will.'

'Simon,' she asked, 'what's the matter with you?'

She bent her head and laid it on his chest. His coat was still wet.

He wiped away her tears with his hand. And then he stroked her, long and tenderly. 'We shall wait, my dear,' he whispered.

He could not sleep that night; he was waiting.

Temple Israel

Minneapolis, Minnesota

In Honor of the Bar Mitzvah of
JOSEPH WILLIAM PRASS
by his Parents,
Mr. & Mrs. David Prass

January 31, 1981